Praise for

OH WILLIAM!

"One proof of Strout's greatness is the sleight of hand with which she injects sneaky subterranean power into seemingly transparent prose. Strout works in the realm of everyday speech, conjuring repetitions, gaps and awkwardness with plain language and forthright diction, yet at the same time unleashing a tidal urgency that seems to come out of nowhere even as it operates in plain sight."

—*The New York Times Book Review*

"So much intimate, fragile, desperate humanness infuses these pages, it's breathtaking. Almost every declaration carries the force of revelation."

—*The Washington Post*

"For all the depths of anger and despair they uncover, and the bitterness they attest to, Strout's works insist on the superabundance of life, the unrealized bliss always immanent in it."

—*The New York Review of Books*

"Being privy to the innermost thoughts of Lucy Barton—and, more to the point, deep inside a book by Strout—makes readers feel safe. We know we're in good hands."

—NPR

"Strout's simple declarative sentences contain continents. Who is better at conveying loneliness, the inability to communicate, to say the deep important things? Who better to illustrate the legacies of imperfect upbringings, of inadequate parents? When William explains that what attracted him to Lucy was her sense of joy, the reader can only agree. This brilliant, compelling, tender novel is—quite simply—a joy."

—*The Boston Globe*

"Strout doesn't dress language up in a tuxedo when a wool sweater will suffice. Other novelists must berate themselves when they see what Strout pulls off without any tacky pyrotechnics."

—*Los Angeles Times*

"The miraculous quality of Strout's fiction is the way she opens up depths with the simplest of touches, and this novel ends with the assurance that the source of love lies less in understanding than in recognition—although it may take a lifetime to learn the difference."

—*The Guardian*

"[Strout] invests us deeply in Lucy's epiphany: Even though we are fueled by presumptions and believe what we want to believe, the truth is always within our sight."

—*Star Tribune*

"[*Oh William!*] serves as a gentle reminder to be emotionally generous with our loved ones and as physically present as possible each and every day of our lives."

—*San Francisco Chronicle*

"Keenly observed and rich with illuminating insight, Strout's tender mercies continue to astound."

—*Esquire*

"The Pulitzer Prize–winning [Oprah's Book Club] author reprises her literary avatar, Lucy Barton, in this radiant—if melancholy—contemplation of marriage, mortality, and love's complexities."

—*Oprah Daily*

"Strout has the remarkable ability to engage audiences immediately with just a few opening sentences. Her marvelous eighth novel, *Oh William!,* is no different, made even more inviting by being the third in her Amgash series. . . . Strout is as sharp as ever—as, no doubt, is Lucy. For all her artless posturing, Lucy's raw, razor-sharp observations about identity and relationships—the adjustments and adaptations necessary for lasting sustainability—propel Strout's narrative toward deeply empathic self-awareness. Along the way, Strout reveals yet another superb story."

—*Shelf Awareness*

"It is, like every Strout novel, completely delightful."

—*Entertainment Weekly*

"It's a quietly wonderful and wise story about, in part, aging, regret, loneliness, difficult people, and finding a measure of contentment in spite of it all."

—*AARP*

"At the core of . . . Strout's best-selling fiction are characters grappling with huge questions about love, loss and family through seemingly ordinary moments. The domestic dramas that fill her books lead to startling revelations about the complexities that accompany marriage, parenthood and growing old. Her new novel is no exception."

—*Time*

"*Oh William!* is, at once, breezy and consequential, in the way that Strout can mention something in passing and also leave a mark."

—*Portland Press Herald*

"What sets Strout apart is the way she describes people's innermost thoughts and the nuances of their feelings. She is an intimate writer with a particular skill for writing about the thoughts that people often brush away or bury, and the result is that you often forget you are reading fiction. You feel like Lucy's confidante."

—*Evening Standard* (U.K.)

"Elizabeth Strout has a novelist's most desirable quality: a distinct voice. Hers is quiet, conversational, intimate. It allows her to move easily between now and then."

—*The Scotsman*

"It's not for nothing that Strout has been compared to Hemingway. In some ways, she betters him."

—*Publishers Weekly* (starred review)

"Strout is a master of reflective stories that are driven more by characters than by events. Her fans will find plenty more to love about Lucy and William."

—*BookPage*

"A masterful, wise, moving, and ultimately uplifting meditation on human existence."

—*Booklist*

"Another skillful, pensive exploration of Strout's fundamental credo: 'We are all mysteries.'"

—*Kirkus Reviews*

"A fine examination of relationships that asks how well one can know someone, even after years together."

—*Library Journal*

BY ELIZABETH STROUT

Oh William!

Olive, Again

Anything Is Possible

My Name Is Lucy Barton

The Burgess Boys

Olive Kitteridge

Abide with Me

Amy and Isabelle

OH WILLIAM!

OH WILLIAM!

A Novel

ELIZABETH STROUT

RANDOM HOUSE
NEW YORK

Oh William! is a work of fiction. Names, characters, places, and incidents are the products of the author's imagination or are used fictitiously. Any resemblance to actual events, locales, or persons, living or dead, is entirely coincidental.

2022 Random House Trade Paperback Edition

Published in the United States by Random House, an imprint and division of Penguin Random House LLC, New York.

RANDOM HOUSE and the HOUSE colophon are registered trademarks of Penguin Random House LLC.

Originally published in hardcover in the United States by Random House, an imprint and division of Penguin Random House LLC, in 2021.

LIBRARY OF CONGRESS CATALOGING-IN-PUBLICATION DATA
Names: Strout, Elizabeth, author.
Title: Oh William! : a novel / Elizabeth Strout
Description: New York : Random House, [2021]
Identifiers: LCCN 2020044757 (print) | LCCN 2020044758 (ebook) | ISBN 9780812989441 (paperback; acid-free paper) | ISBN 9780812989458 (ebook)
Classification: LCC PS3569.T736 O38 2021 (print) | LCC PS3569.T736 (ebook) | DDC 813/.54—dc23
LC record available at https://lccn.loc.gov/2020044757
LC ebook record available at https://lccn.loc.gov/2020044758

Printed in the United States of America on acid-free paper

randomhousebooks.com

2 4 6 8 9 7 5 3 1

Book design by Dana Leigh Blanchette

This book is dedicated to my husband,
Jim Tierney

And to anyone who needs it—this is for you

OH WILLIAM!

I would like to say a few things about my first husband, William.

William has lately been through some very sad events—many of us have—but I would like to mention them, it feels almost a compulsion; he is seventy-one years old now.

My second husband, David, died last year, and in my grief for him I have felt grief for William as well. Grief is such a—oh, it is such a *solitary* thing; this is the terror of it, I think. It is like sliding down the outside of a really long glass building while nobody sees you.

But it is William I want to speak of here.

═

His name is William Gerhardt, and when we married I took his last name, even though at the time it was not fashionable to do so. My college roommate said, "Lucy, you're taking his name? I thought you were a feminist." And I told her that I did not care about being a feminist; I told her I did not want to be me anymore. At that time I felt that I was *tired* of being me, I had spent my whole life not wanting to be me—this is what I thought then—and so I took his name and became Lucy Gerhardt for eleven years, but it did not ever feel right to me, and almost immediately after William's mother died I went to the motor vehicle place to get my own name back on my driver's license, even though it was more difficult than I had thought it would be; I had to go back and bring in some court documents; but I did.

I became Lucy Barton again.

We were married for almost twenty years before I left him and we have two daughters, and we have been friendly for a long time now—how, I am not sure exactly. There are many terrible stories of divorce, but except for the separation itself ours is not one of them. Sometimes I thought I would die from the pain of our separating, and the pain it caused my girls, but I did not die, and I am here, and so is William.

Because I am a novelist, I have to write this almost like a novel, but it is true—as true as I can make it. And I want to say—oh, it is difficult to know what to say! But when I report something about William it is because he told it to me or because I saw it with my own eyes.

So I will start this story when William was sixty-nine years old, which is less than two years ago now.

═

A visual:

Recently William's lab assistant had taken to calling William "Einstein," and William seemed to get a real kick out of that. I do not think William looks like Einstein at all, but I take the young woman's point. William has a very full mustache with gray in its whiteness, but it is sort of a trimmed mustache and his hair is full and white. It is cut, but it does stick out from his head. He is a tall man, and he dresses very well. And he does not have that vaguely crazy look that Einstein, to my mind, seemed to have. William's face is often closed with an unyielding pleasantness, except for once in a very great while when he throws his head back in real laughter; I have not seen him do that for a long time. His eyes are brown and they have stayed large; not everyone's eyes stay large as they get older, but William's eyes have.

—

Now—

Every morning William would rise in his spacious apartment on Riverside Drive. Picture him—throwing aside the fluffy quilt with its dark blue cotton cover, his wife still asleep in their king-size bed, and going into the bathroom. He would, every morning, be stiff. But he had exercises and he did them, going out into the living room, lying on his back on the large black-and-red rug with the antique chandelier above him, pedaling his legs in the air as though on a bicycle, then stretching them this way and that. Then he'd move to the large maroon chair by the window that looked out over the Hudson River, and he would read the news on his laptop there. At some point Estelle would emerge from the bedroom and wave to him sleepily and then she would wake their daughter, Bridget, who was ten, and after William took his shower the three of them had breakfast in the kitchen at the round table; William enjoyed the routine of this, and his daughter was a chatty girl, which he liked as well; it was as though listening to a bird, he once said, and her mother was chatty also.

After he left the apartment he walked across Central Park and then took the subway downtown, where he got off at Fourteenth Street and walked the remaining distance to New York University; he enjoyed this daily walking even though he noticed that he was not as fast as the young people who bumped past him with their bags of food, or their strollers with two kids, or their spandex tights and earbuds in their ears, their yoga mats on a piece of elastic slung over their shoulders. He took heart in the fact that he could pass many people—the old man with a walker, or a woman who used a cane, or even just a person his age who seemed to move more slowly than he did—and this made him feel healthy and alive and almost invulnerable in a world of constant traffic. He was proud that he walked more than ten thousand steps a day.

William felt (almost) invulnerable, is what I am saying here.

Some days on these morning walks he would think, Oh God I could be *that man*—! over there in the wheelchair sitting in the morning sun in Central Park, an aide on a bench typing on her cellphone as the man's head dropped forward to his chest, or he could be *that one*—! with an arm twisted from a stroke, a gait uneven— But then William would think: No, I am not those people.

And he was not those people. He was, as I have said, a tall man, to whom age had not added extra weight (except for a small potbelly you could barely see with his clothes on), a man who still had his hair, white now but full, and he was—William. And he had a wife, his third, twenty-two years younger than he was. And that was no small thing.

—

But at night, he often had terrors.

William told me this one morning—not quite two years ago—when we met for coffee on the Upper East Side. We met at a diner on the corner of Ninety-first Street and Lexington Avenue; William has a lot of money and he gives a lot of it away and one place he gives it to is a hospital for adolescent children near where I live, and in the past when he had an early-morning meeting there he would call me and we would meet briefly for coffee on this corner. On this day—it was March, a few months before William was to turn seventy—we sat at a table in the corner of this diner; on the windows were painted shamrocks for St. Patrick's Day, and I thought—I did think this—that William looked more tired than usual. I have often thought that William gets better-looking with age. The full white hair gives him an air of distinction; he wears it a little bit longer than he used to and it rises slightly from his head, with his big drooping mustache to counter it, and his cheekbones have emerged more, his eyes are still dark; and it is a tiny bit odd, because he will watch you fully—pleasantly—but then every so often his eyes become briefly penetrating. So what is he penetrating with that look? I have never known.

That day in the diner, when I asked him "So how *are*

you, William?," I expected him to answer as he always does, which is to say in an ironical tone "Why, I am perfectly fine, thank you, Lucy," but this morning he just said "I'm okay." He was wearing a long black overcoat, which he removed and folded over the chair next to him before sitting down. His suit was tailor-made, since meeting Estelle he had been having his suits tailor-made, and so it fit his shoulders perfectly; it was dark gray and his shirt was pale blue and his tie was red; he looked solemn. He folded his arms across his chest, which is what he often does. "You're looking nice," I said, and he said, "Thanks." (I think William has never told me that I am looking good, or pretty, or even well, in all the times we have seen each other over the years, and the truth is that I have always hoped he will.) He ordered our coffee and his eyes flitted about the place while he tugged lightly on his mustache. He spoke about our girls for a while—he was afraid that Becka, the younger, was mad at him; she had been sort of—vaguely—unpleasant to him on the phone when he had simply called to chat with her one day, and I told him that he just had to give her space, she was settling herself into her marriage—we spoke like that for a bit—and then William looked at me and said, "Button, I want to tell you something." He leaned forward briefly. "I've been having these awful terrors in the middle of the night."

When he uses my pet name from our past it means that he is present in some way he is so often not, and I am always touched when he calls me that.

I said, "You mean nightmares?"

He cocked his head as though considering this and said, "No. I wake up. It's in the dark when things come to me." He added, "I've never had this sort of thing before. But they're terrifying, Lucy. They terrify me."

William leaned forward again and set his coffee cup down.

I watched him, and then I asked, "Is there some kind of different medication that you're taking?"

He scowled slightly and said, "No."

So I said, "Well, try taking a sleeping pill."

And he said, "I have never taken a sleeping pill," which did not surprise me. But he said that his wife did; Estelle took a variety of pills, he had stopped trying to understand the handful she took at night. "I'm taking my pills now," she would say gaily, and in half an hour she was asleep. He didn't mind that, he said. But pills were not for him. Still, in four hours he would often be awake and the terrors often began.

"Tell me," I said.

And he did, glancing at me only occasionally as though he were still inside these terrors.

—

One terror: It was not nameable, but it had something to do with his mother. His mother—her name was Catherine—had died many, many years earlier, but in this nighttime terror he would feel her presence, but it was not a good presence and this surprised him because he had loved her. William had been an only child, and he had always understood his mother's (quietly) ferocious love for him.

To get over this terror while he lay awake in bed next to his sleeping wife—he told me this that day, and it kind of killed me—he would think of *me*. He would think about the fact that I was out there alive, right now—I was alive—and this gave him comfort. Because he knew if he had to, he said, arranging the spoon on the saucer of the coffee cup—even though he would never want to do this in the middle of the night—he knew if he *should* have to, that I would take a call from him. He told me my presence is what he found to be the greatest comfort and so he would fall back to sleep.

"Of course you can always call me," I said.

And William rolled his eyes. "I *know* that. That's my *point*," he said.

Another terror: This had to do with Germany and his father, who had died when William was fourteen. His father had come from Germany as a prisoner of war—World War II—and been sent to work on the potato fields in Maine, where he met William's mother; she was married to the potato farmer. This might have been William's worst terror, because his father had been fighting on the side of the Nazis, and this fact would visit William in the night sometimes and cause him terror—he would see very clearly the concentration camps—we had visited them on a trip to Germany—and he would see the rooms where people were gassed, and then he would have to get up and move into the living room and put the light on and sit on the couch and look out the window at the river, and no amount of thinking about me or anything else could help with these terrors. They did not come as frequently as the ones with his mother, but when they did come they were very bad.

One more: This had to do with death. It had to do with a sense of leaving, he could feel himself almost leaving the world and he did not believe in any afterlife and so this filled him on certain nights with a kind of terror. But he could stay in bed usually, though sometimes he got up and went into the living room and sat in the large maroon chair by the window and read a book—he liked biographies—until he felt he could return to sleep.

"How long have you been having these?" I asked. The diner we sat in had been there for years and was crowded at this time of day; four white paper napkins had been tossed onto the table after our coffee had been brought.

William looked out the window and seemed to be watching an old woman who was walking by with her walker with a seat in it; she moved slowly, bent over, her coat blowing behind her in the wind. "A few months, I think," he said.

"You mean they just started out of the blue?"

And he looked at me then; his eyebrows were getting shaggy above his dark eyes, and he said, "I think they did." After a moment he sat back and said, "It must be just that I'm getting older."

"Maybe," I said. But I was not sure this was the reason. William has always been a mystery to me—and to our girls as well. I said, tentatively, "Do you want to see anyone to talk to about them?"

"God, no," he said, and that part of him was not a mystery to me, I thought he would probably say that. "But it's awful," he added.

"Oh Pillie," I said, using my pet name for him from so long ago. "I'm so sorry."

"I wish we'd never taken that trip to Germany," he said. He picked up one of the napkins and swiped at his nose with it. Then he ran his hand down over—almost reflexively, as he often does—his mustache. "And I really wish we'd never gone to Dachau. I keep picturing those—those crematoriums." He added, glancing at me, "You were smart not to go into them."

I was surprised that William remembered that I had not gone into the gas chamber or the crematoriums that summer we went to Germany. I did not go into them because even back then I knew myself well enough to know I should not do that; and I did not. William's mother had died the year before, and the girls had been nine and ten; they were in summer camp together for two weeks and so we flew to Germany—I had asked only that we take separate flights, I was that scared of us both dying in a plane crash and leaving the girls orphans, which was silly, I saw later, because we could easily have both died on the autobahn as the cars whizzed past us—and we went there to find out what we could about William's father, who had died, as I have said, when William was fourteen; he died in a hospital in Massachusetts from peritonitis, he was having a polyp removed from his intestine and there was a puncture and he died. We went to Germany that summer because William had come into a great deal of money a few years earlier, it turned out his grandfather had profited on the war, and when William turned thirty-five he came into the money from a trust, and this was a source of distress for William, and so we had flown over together and seen the old man, he was *very* old, and met two aunts of William's, they were polite but cold, I felt. And the old man, his grandfather, had small glittery eyes and I disliked him especially. The trip left us both unhappy.

"You know what?" I said. "I think the nighttime stuff will start to disappear. It's a phase of some kind—it will work its way out."

William looked at me again and said, "It's the ones of Catherine that really get to me. I have no idea what they're about." William has always spoken of his mother by her first name; he called her that as well. I can never remember his calling her "Mom." And then he put his napkin on the table and stood up. "I have to get going," he said. "Always nice to see you, Button."

I said, "William! How long have you been drinking coffee?"

"Years," he said. He bent to kiss me and his cheek felt cold; his mustache bristled just slightly against my cheek.

I turned to glance out the window at him, and he was walking quickly along to the subway; he was not walking as erect as he usually did. A little bit, the sight of him then broke my heart. But I was used to that feeling—I had it almost every time after I saw him.

During the days, William went to work in his lab. He is a parasitologist and he had taught microbiology at New York University for many years; they still allowed him his lab and one student assistant; he does not teach classes anymore. About not teaching: He was surprised to find he did not miss it—he told me this recently—it turned out he had felt trepidation every time he stood before the class, and it was not until his teaching stopped that he understood that that had been true.

Why does this touch me? I guess because I never knew; and because he never knew too.

And so now he went to work every day from ten in the morning until four in the afternoon, and he wrote papers and did research and supervised the assistant who worked in his lab. Every so often—a couple of times a year, I think—he went to a conference and would deliver a paper to other scientists who worked in his field.

═

Two things happened to William after we met at the diner, and I will get to those soon.

Let me first just speak briefly of his marriages:

Me, Lucy.

William had been the teaching assistant for my biology class—he was a graduate student—my sophomore year at a college right outside of Chicago; this is how we met. He was—he still is, of course—seven years older than I am.

I came from terribly bleak poverty. This is part of the story, and I wish it was not, but it is. I came from a very tiny house in the middle of Illinois—before we moved into the tiny house we had lived in a garage until I was eleven. When we lived in the garage we had a small chemical toilet, but it was often breaking, making my father furious; there was an outhouse we had to walk through part of a field to get to; my mother had once told me a story of a man who had been killed and had his head chopped off and his head had been put in some outhouse. This scared me just unbelievably, I never picked up the cover of that outhouse toilet without thinking I saw the eyeballs of a man, and I would often go to the bathroom in the field if no one was around, although in the winter that was more difficult. We had a chamber pot as well.

Our place was in the middle of acres and acres of cornfields and soybean fields. I have an older brother and an older sister, and we had our two parents back then. But very bad things happened in the garage and then later in that tiny house. I have written about some of the things that happened in that house, and I don't care really to write any more about it. But we were really terribly poor. So I will just say this: When I was seventeen years old I won a full scholarship to that college right outside of Chicago, no one in my family had ever gone past high school. My guidance counselor drove me to the college, her name was Mrs. Nash; she picked me up at ten in the morning on a Saturday in late August.

The night before, I had asked my mother what I should pack in, and she said, "I don't give a damn what you pack in." So eventually I took two paper grocery bags that I found under the kitchen sink, and also a box from my father's truck, and I put my few clothes in the grocery bags and the box. The next morning my mother drove away at nine-thirty and I went running out into the long dirt driveway and I yelled, "Mom! Mommy!" But she drove away, turning onto the road where the hand-painted sign said SEWING AND ALTERATIONS. My brother and sister were not there, I don't remember where they were. A little before ten o'clock, as I started to go to the door, my father said, "You have everything you need, Lucy?" And when I looked at him he had tears in his eyes, and I said, "Yes, Daddy." But I had no idea what I needed at college. My father hugged me, and he said, "I think I'll stay in the house," and I understood, and I said, "Okay, I'll go wait outside," and I stood in the driveway with the grocery bags and the box with my few clothes in it until Mrs. Nash drove up.

From the moment I got into Mrs. Nash's car my life changed. Oh, it changed!

And then I met William.

I want to say right up front: I still get very frightened. I think this must be because of what happened to me in my youth, but I get very scared very easily. For example, almost every night when the sun goes down, I still get scared. Or sometimes I will just feel fear as though something terrible will happen to me. Although when I first met William I did not know this about myself, it all felt—oh, I guess it just felt like me.

But when I was leaving my marriage to William I went to a woman psychiatrist, she was a lovely woman, and she asked me a number of questions that first visit and I answered them, and she told me then, slipping her glasses up to the top of her head, a name for what was the matter with me. "Lucy—you have full-blown post-traumatic stress disorder." In a way, this helped me. I mean the way naming things can be helpful.

I left William just as the girls were going off to college. I became a writer. I mean I was always a writer, but I began to publish books—I had published one book—but I began to publish more books, this is what I mean.

Joanne.

About a year after our marriage ended, William married a woman he had had an affair with for six years. It could have been longer than six years, I don't know. This woman, her name was Joanne, was a friend of both of ours since college. She looked the opposite of me; I mean she was tall and had long dark hair; and she was a quiet person. After she and William married, she became very bitter, he had not expected that (he told me this part recently), because she felt she had given up her childbearing years in being his mistress—though this was not a word used by either of them, it is the word I am using now—and so when they settled into their marriage she felt always upset by his two daughters that he had had with me, even though Joanne had known them since they were very young. He found it distasteful to go to the marriage counselor with Joanne. He thought the woman counselor was intelligent, he thought Joanne was not especially intelligent, although it was not until his time in that office, with its dismal gray-cushioned couch, and the woman sitting across from them in a swivel chair, with no natural light in the room, the one window having a rice paper shade to block out the view of the building shaft it looked upon, it was not until he came there that he understood this about Joanne, that her intelligence was moderate and that his attraction to her all those years had simply been the fact that she was not his wife, Lucy. Me.

He had endured the counseling for eight weeks. "You only want what you can't have," Joanne had said to him, quietly, one of their last nights together, and he—his arms crossed in front of him, is how I picture him—had said nothing. The marriage lasted seven years.

I hate her. Joanne. I hate her.

—

Estelle.

His third marriage is to a gracious (much younger) woman, and with her he fathered a child, although he had told her repeatedly when they met that he would have no more children. When Estelle told him that she was pregnant, she said, "You could have had a vasectomy," and he never forgot that. He could have. And he had not. He realized that she had gotten herself pregnant on purpose, and he immediately went and had a vasectomy—without telling Estelle. When the little girl was born he discovered this about being an older father to a young child: He loved her. He loved her very much, but the sight of her, especially when she was young, and then even more as she grew, reminded him almost constantly of his two daughters that he had had with me, and when he heard of men who had had two families—and he supposed he himself had—and who had more time with the younger children and the older children resented the younger ones and so on and so forth, he always secretly felt, Well, that is not me. Because his daughter Bridget, daughter of Estelle, made him almost crumple at times with a nostalgic love that seeped up from the depths of him for his first two daughters, who were by then well over thirty years old.

When he spoke to Estelle on the phone during the day there were a few times he called her "Lucy," and Estelle always laughed and took it well.

═

The next time I saw William was at his seventieth birthday party, thrown by Estelle for him in their apartment. It was toward the end of May, and it was a clear night but chilly. My husband, David, had been invited as well, but he was a cellist and played in the Philharmonic and he had a concert that night and so I went, and our daughters, Chrissy and Becka, were there with their husbands. I had been to the apartment twice before, an engagement party for Becka and a birthday party for Chrissy another time, and I never liked the place. It is cavernous, room after room unfolding as you go in, but I found it to be dark, and it was overdone to my taste, but almost everything is overdone to my taste. I have known others who came from poverty and they have often compensated by having rather gorgeous apartments, but the apartment I lived in with David—and still live in—is a simple place; David came from poverty too.

In any event, Estelle came from Larchmont, New York, and she came from money, and between the two of them Estelle and William had made a home for themselves that left me quietly baffled because it did not feel like a home, it felt more like what it was—room after room of wooden floors—with nice rugs—and wooden sidings on the door-ways, just a lot of dark, dark wood, it seemed to me, and then the chandeliers here and there, and a kitchen that was as big as our bedroom—I mean for a New York kitchen it was enormous, with lots of chrome in it and yet that dark wood as well, wooden cupboards and things. A round wooden table in the kitchen and, in the dining room, a long, much bigger wooden table. And mirrors placed around. I knew that it was expensively appointed, the maroon chair by the window was a big upholstered thing, and the couch was a dark brown with velvet cushions on it.

I just never understood the place, is what I am saying.

The night of William's birthday party I stopped at a corner market and bought three sleeves of white tulips to take there, and remembering this I think how true it is that we choose gifts that we ourselves love. The apartment was filled with people, although not as many as I might have thought, but it makes me nervous, that kind of thing. You start a conversation with someone and another person comes along and you have to interrupt yourself, and then you see their eyes looking around the room as you talk—you know how it is. It was stressful, but the girls—our girls—were really very darling and they were nice to Bridget, I noticed that, and I was glad to see it, because when they speak of her to me they are not always generous, and of course I take their side, that she is a bubblehead and shallow, that sort of thing, but she is just a girl, and a pretty one, and she knows it. And she is also rich. None of these things are her fault, I tell myself that each time I see her. She is no relative of mine. But she is related to our girls, and so that is that.

There were a number of older men who had worked at NYU with William, and their wives, some of them I had been acquainted with from years back, and it was all okay. But tiresome. There was a woman named Pam Carlson who knew William many years ago—they had worked in some lab together—and she was drunk, but I sort of remembered her from way back and she was very talkative to me at the party; she kept talking about her first husband, Bob Burgess. Did I remember him? And I said I was sorry but I didn't. And Pam, who was very stylish that night with a dress I would never have thought to wear—I mean it fit her snugly though she pulled it off, a sleeveless black dress that I thought remarkably low-cut, but her arms were skinny and looked as though she worked out at the gym even though she must have been my age, sixty-three, and she was kind of touching in her drunken way; she nodded toward her husband, who was standing at a distance, and said she loved him, but she found herself thinking of Bob a lot, did I find that to be true with William as well? And I said, "Sometimes," and then I excused myself and moved away from her. I had the feeling that I was almost drunk enough myself that I could have really talked to Pam about William, and when it was that I especially missed him, but I did not want to do that, so I went over to where Becka was standing, and she rubbed my arm and said, "Hi Mommy." And then Estelle gave a toast; she was wearing a dress with sequins implanted in the material and it also draped very nicely around her shoulders; she is an attractive woman with kind of wild brownish red hair which I've always liked, and she gave this toast and I thought: She did that so well. But she is an actress by trade.

Becka whispered, "Oh Mom, I have to give a toast!" And I said, "No, you don't. Why do you think that?"

But then Chrissy gave a toast, and it was really well done, I cannot remember it all, but it was as good as—if not better than—Estelle's. I remember only that she spoke—at one point—of her father's work, and all that he had done to help so many students. Chrissy is tall like her father, and she has a composure to her; she always has. Becka looked at me with fear in her brown eyes, and then she murmured, "Oh Mommy, okay." And she said, raising her glass, "Dad, my toast is that I love you. That is my toast for you. I love you." And people clapped and I hugged her, and Chrissy came over and the girls were nice to each other, as they—I think—almost always are; they have always been—to my mind—almost unnaturally close, they live two blocks from each other in Brooklyn, and I talked with their husbands for a few more minutes; Chrissy's husband is in finance, which is a little strange for William and me to think about, only because William is a scientist and I am a writer and so we don't know people who work in that world, and he is a shrewd man, you can see it in his eyes, and Becka's husband is a poet, oh dear God the poor fellow, and I think he is self-centered. And then William came over and we all chatted easily for a while until someone called him away, and he bent down and said, "Thank you for coming, Lucy. It was good of you to come."

═

At times in our marriage I loathed him. I saw, with a kind of dull disc of dread in my chest, that with his pleasant distance, his mild expressions, he was unavailable. But worse. Because beneath his height of pleasantness there lurked a juvenile crabbiness, a scowl that flickered across his soul, a pudgy little boy with his lower lip thrust forward who blamed this person and that person—he blamed me, I felt this often; he was blaming me for something that had nothing to do with our present lives, and he blamed me even as he called me "Sweetheart," making my coffee—back then he never drank coffee but he made me a cup each morning—setting it down before me martyr-like.

Keep the stupid coffee, I wanted to cry out sometimes, I'll make my own coffee. But I took it from him, touching his hand. "Thanks, sweetheart," I would say, and we would begin another day.

═

As I rode home that night in a taxi, across town and through the Park, I thought about Estelle. She was so pretty, with her reddish-brown wild hair and twinkling eyes, and she was very good-natured. She was, William had told me once, never depressed, and I thought it was unconsciously mean of him to tell me that, since I had been depressed at times during our marriage, but tonight I thought, Well, I'm glad she's never depressed. She had been floating around as a stage actress when she met him. William had seen her in only one play, they were married by then, and the play was called *The Steelman's Grave,* in a small off-off-Broadway production, and my husband and I went to see it with William one night. I had been aghast to see that when Estelle was on stage and not speaking, her eyes looked involuntarily to the audience as though searching for someone. Since that time she had gone to countless auditions for which she practiced at home, walking through their large living room doing Gertrude or Hedda Gabler or any other kind of role, and she remained cheerful when she did not get the parts. But she had done a few commercials, there had been one on a local New York television station where she was talking about deodorant. "It's the right one for me," she said, adding, with a wink, "And I bet"—pointing her finger toward the camera—"it will be the right one for you."

People often said to them that they were a charming couple. And Estelle was a good, if somewhat scattered, mother. William thought this, and I did too. Bridget was scattered as well, and they looked alike, this mother and daughter, people also seemed charmed by that. One day—William told me this—he had watched them walking down a sidewalk together, they had just come from a clothing shop in the Village, and he was taken with how similar they were in their gestures as they laughed with each other. Estelle had seen him and she waved extravagantly, which is something William does not do, and she jokingly chastised him that day. "When a wife is so happy to see her husband, she would *like* to think he was happy to see her too."

═

Recently, sitting in my apartment, gazing through the window at the view of the city—we have (I have) a lovely view of the city and of the East River too—but as I was looking at the lights of the city and the Empire State Building way in the distance, I thought of Mrs. Nash, the guidance counselor from my school who drove me to college that first day—oh I loved her! As we drove along she suddenly pulled off the turnpike and drove to a shopping mall, and tapping my arm she said, "Get out, get out," and we got out and went into the mall and then she put a hand on my shoulder and looked into my eyes and said, "In ten years, Lucy, you can pay me back, okay?" And she bought me some clothes: She bought me a number of long-sleeve T-shirts in many different colors, and two skirts and two blouses, one was a pretty peasant kind of blouse, and what I remember most and loved her for the most was the underwear she bought me, a small pile of the prettiest underwear I had ever seen, and she bought me a pair of jeans that fit me. And she bought me a suitcase! It was beige with red trim, and when we got back to the car she said, "I have an idea. Let's put everything in here." And she opened her trunk and put the suitcase in the trunk and opened the suitcase, and then she so carefully and kindly took off each price tag with the tiniest little scissors I had ever seen—I have since learned they were manicure scissors—and we put all my stuff into the suitcase. She did that, Mrs. Nash. In ten years she had died; it was a car accident that killed her, so I never paid her back and I have never forgotten her ever. (Every single time I went shopping with Catherine, I thought of that day with Mrs. Nash.) When we got to the college that day I said to Mrs. Nash, sort of jokingly, "Can I pretend you're my mother?" And she looked surprised and then said, "Of course you can, Lucy!" And even though I never called her Mom, when she went into the dorm with me she was nice to people and I think they thought she was my mother.

I will always—oh, always!—I will always love that woman.

═

A few weeks later William called from the lab—he tended to call me when he was at work—and thanked me again for coming to the party. "Did you have a good time?" he asked. And I told him that I had; I told him about talking to Pam Carlson and how she wanted to talk about her first husband, Bob something. As I spoke I was watching the river, a huge red barge was going by, pushed by a tugboat.

"Bob Burgess," said William. "He was a nice guy. She left him because he couldn't have kids."

"Did he work with you as well?" I asked.

"No. He was a public defender or something. His brother was Jim Burgess—remember the Wally Packer trial? That was his brother who defended him."

"It *was*?" I said. Wally Packer was a soul singer accused of killing his girlfriend, and Jim Burgess got him off. At the time, this was many years ago, the trial was huge; it was televised and the whole country seemed involved with it. I always thought Wally Packer was innocent, I remember that, and I thought Jim Burgess was a hero.

So we discussed that for a few minutes; William said what he had said before, that I was an idiot to think Wally Packer was innocent. And I let it go.

And then I suddenly asked William, "Did *you* enjoy the party?"

He said, after a pause, "I guess so."

I said, "What do you mean, you guess so? Estelle put a lot of work into that party."

"She hired a caterer, Lucy."

"So what? She still put it all together." The barge was moving quickly; it always surprises me how quickly they can move, it must have been empty, it was riding high, I could see a lot of the black underneath of it.

"Yeah, yeah, I know, I know. No, it was a great party. I have to go now."

"Pill," I said. "Let me just ask you. How are your nights going? You know, your nighttime terrors?"

And I could hear in his voice that this was why he had called me. "Oh Lucy," he said, "I had one last night—well, it was around three o'clock this morning. About Catherine—It's really weird, I can't describe it exactly. I mean, it's like she's hovering there." He paused and then said, "I think I might have to take a drug. It's getting really tough." He added, "It's like Catherine is *with* me, I mean, her presence, and it's just—it's just not good, Lucy."

"Oh Pillie," I said. "Man, I'm just so sorry."

We talked a bit more, and then we hung up.

But here is something I had not thought of until William called and spoke to me of the party:

The night of the party I had walked into their kitchen with a glass to put down and to say goodbye to Estelle, who was walking slightly ahead of me, and there was a man in the kitchen, leaning against the counter, he was a friend of hers, I had met him before, and I heard Estelle say to him quietly, "Are you bored to death?" And then she turned and saw me and exclaimed, "Oh Lucy, it was so fun to see you again!" And the man said the same—he had always seemed like a nice fellow, another theater person—and I chatted with Estelle and we kissed on the cheek and I left. But I had not liked the tone of her voice with the man; there was an intimacy to it, and it implied—perhaps—that she herself was bored, and this was a thing I did not care for. It was a tiny *ping* I felt, I guess is what I am saying. But I had forgotten about it until then.

Also (I suddenly remembered this too), the tulips I had brought were still in their wrappings on the kitchen counter.

This did not especially disturb me; the party had arrangements from a florist, it had been silly to think that tulips from a corner market would be wanted there.

It was the voice of Estelle that lingered.

My husband became ill early that summer, and he died in November. That is all I am able to say about that right now, except that it had been a very different marriage from my marriage to William.

Except I do need to say this: My husband's namc was David Abramson and he was—oh, how can I tell you what he was? He was *him*! We were—we really were—kind of made for each other, except that seems a terrifically trite thing to say but— Oh, I cannot say any more right now.

But there is this: Both with the discovery of David's illness, and then again with his death, it was William I called first. I think—but I don't remember—that I must have said something like "Oh William, help me." Because he did. He got my husband to a different doctor—a better one, I do believe—although there was nothing any doctor could do at that point.

And then, with the death, William helped me again.

He helped me with some of the business aspects—there is so much to do when a person dies, different credit cards to close, and bank accounts and so many computer passwords—and William told me to let Chrissy organize the service, which was very smart of William; Chrissy did all of that.

It was Becka who came and stayed with me those first nights; she did my crying for me at that time. She wept and wept with the abandonment of a child, then flung herself onto the couch, and a few minutes later she said something—I have no idea what—and we both started to laugh. She is like that, dear Becka. She made me laugh, and then she had to go home, as she should have.

At David's service in a funeral home in the city—which was then, and is now, all a blur to me—I do remember Becka whispering to me, "Dad wishes he could sit up here with us."

"He *said* that to you?" I asked, turning to look at her, and she nodded solemnly. Poor William, I thought.

Poor William.

═

At Christmastime, Estelle called and asked me if I wanted to come and have Christmas Day with them. I said it was really kind of her to ask me, but no, I was going to be with the girls, and as soon as I said that I remembered Becka's saying how William had wanted to sit up front with us during the service, and it did go through my mind that William might have wanted to spend Christmas with the girls and me, that maybe he had asked Estelle if we could be included. But he had had Christmas with Estelle and her mother for years now, and Bridget, of course; Estelle's mother was almost William's age. I have an image of their apartment all done up for the holidays with a big Christmas tree, Becka had told me about it; she said, wryly, that it was as festive as Macy's. And I said, "Not as expensive as Saks?" And we had laughed. And there was a yearly Christmas party they went to at night nearby in their neighborhood; William had always enjoyed that.

"I understand," Estelle said. "But just know we're thinking of you, Lucy. Okay?"

"Thank you," I said. "Thank you so much."

"We know it has to be hard with David gone," she said. "Oh Lucy—I feel so bad for you."

"I'm okay," I said. "Don't worry. But thank you," I said again. "I really do appreciate it."

"Okay." Estelle hesitated. "Okay," she said again. "Well, bye-bye."

==

So a new year began. And in rather quick succession, two events happened to William. But let me mention just a few more things first.

==

In January, William told me—on the phone from his lab, and after we had spoken of the girls—that for Christmas he had given Estelle an expensive vase that she had admired in a store one day. And she had given him a subscription to an online thing where you could find out about your ancestors. I could tell by the way he told me that he had been disappointed with the gift. Gifts have always been important to William in a way I have never understood. "But that was smart of her," I said. "What a good idea." I said, "You know almost nothing about your mother, William, this could be good." I do remember that I said that. And he only said "Yeah. I guess." This was the William who was tiresome to me, the petulant boy beneath his distinguished and pleasant demeanor. But I did not care, he was no longer mine. And when I hung up I thought: Thank God. And I meant about him being no longer mine.

==

But here is one thing I would have told the Pam Carlson woman, had I stayed and talked with her at that party for William: A few years before David died we went to Pennsylvania for his nephew's marriage. David had been raised a Hasidic Jew right outside of Chicago, and he had left that community when he was nineteen; they ostracized him then, he had had no contact with any of his family until just recently, when his sister got in touch with him, so I did not know her well; she seemed a stranger to me because she was. We went on the train and then his sister picked us up and we drove through the dark for half an hour to a hotel in the middle of nowhere. It had snowed the night before and I sat in the backseat and stared out the window at all the darkness going by, the rare house could be seen and, every so often, various stores—one with a sign on it that said GOING OUT OF BUSINESS *FOREVER*—or storage-looking places, and my heart was so heavy. Because it all made me think of William and how when we were young and I was in college we would drive through the night from Chicago back East to see his mother and we drove through places like this, snowy areas that looked forlorn, but I had felt so happy with him, I felt *snug* with him. William had no siblings, as I have said—and in a way, at that point, neither did I—and there was, that night as I drove with my current husband and his sister, a strong memory of coziness, because William and I had been a world unto ourselves, and I remembered one drive back East when he had said I could throw my peach pit out the window, and I had thrown it out *his* window for some reason, he was driving, and the peach pit hit him in the face, and I remember we laughed and laughed, as if it were the funniest thing that had ever happened. And then also a few years later we would drive to Newton, Massachusetts, to see his mother with our baby girls tucked into their car seats, and there was still that sense of coziness. But that night in the backseat of the car as we passed the snowy acres of land and I sort of heard my husband and his sister speaking quietly of their childhood, passing by billboards that said HIT BY A CAR? CALL HHR, I thought to myself: William is the only person I ever felt safe with. He is the only home I ever had.

I might have told Pam Carlson that had I not walked away.

═

About my former mother-in-law, Catherine, I would like to say this:

When I first became engaged to William she asked me with excitement, it was almost the first thing she asked me, she was on the telephone, "Will you call me Mom?" And I said, "I'll try." But I could never do it. I could only call her Catherine, which is what William did. Catherine Cole had been her maiden name, and sometimes William called her that with a slight tone of irony and a twinkle in his eye. "Catherine Cole, what have you been up to these days?"

We loved her. Oh, we *loved* her; she seemed central to our marriage. She was vibrant; her face was often filled with light. A college friend of mine who met her for the first time said afterward, "Catherine is the most immediately likeable person I have ever met."

I thought her house was remarkable; it was on a tree-lined street in Newton, Massachusetts, with other houses nearby. The first time I saw it, sunshine was streaming through the kitchen windows and the kitchen was large with a white table in it, and it shone with cleanliness. The counters were white and a large African violet sat on one of the window shelves over the sink. The kitchen faucet was a long thing that arched out over the sink, and it sparkled a silver color. I thought I had stepped into heaven. Catherine's entire house was clean; the wooden floors in the living room shone a honey color, and the bedrooms had curtains that were white and starched-looking. Never did I think I could live like that. It did not occur to me. But that *she* lived like that! Really, I could not get over it.

—

I need to say this, though:

I wrote about it in an earlier book, but I need to explain it more, which is that when I first met William and heard that his mother had been married to a potato farmer in Maine, I thought—because I did not know about potato farms in Maine—that she would have been rather poor. But this was not the case. Catherine's first husband, the potato farmer Clyde Trask, had run a good and successful farm, and he had also been a politician; he was a Republican state legislator in Maine for many years. And Catherine's second husband, William's father, when he came to America after the war, became a civil engineer. So Catherine was not poor. And when I met her I was surprised at the elegance of her home. I think she had ended up rather high on the social scale. I have never fully understood the whole class business in America, though, because I came from the very bottom of it, and when that happens it never really leaves you. I mean I have never really gotten over it, my beginnings, the poverty, I guess is what I mean.

But Catherine, when I first met her, would introduce me to her friends, and she would say quietly with her hand on my arm, "This is Lucy. Lucy comes from nothing." I wrote about that in a previous book.

—

In Catherine's living room was a long couch, a sort of tangerine color, and Catherine would sometimes be stretched out on the couch if we arrived without her knowing, which we did sometimes because William liked surprising her. "Oh! Oh!" she would say, scrambling up, "Come give me a hug," and we would go to her and then she would take us to the kitchen and give us food, always talking, always asking how we were, telling William he needed to have his hair cut. "You're such a handsome boy," she would say, putting her hand on his chin. "Why can't we see more of you? Get rid of that mustache." She was light itself. Mostly she was. Once in a while she seemed more subdued and she would say, almost laughingly, "Oh, I have the blues," and William said she had always been like that, not to worry, but even when she was subdued she was still kind, always asking about the details of our lives; our friends' names she knew and she would ask about them too. "How is Joanne?" I remember her asking. "Has she found a husband yet?" And then she said, winking at me, "She's a little dour, that one."

She would sit at the table and watch us eat. "Tell me everything!" she would say. And so we did. We told her about our life in New York City, we told her about the downstairs neighbor whose wife was much younger than he was and she didn't seem to like him, and I told her how the old man one day had blocked the stairs and wouldn't let me get past until I had kissed him. "Lucy!" she said. "That's horrible!

Don't you ever kiss him again!" And I told her I had to, and she said, "No. You do not have to." I said it had just been a peck on the cheek, but it had made me feel weird. "Of course it made you feel weird!" She shook her head and ran her hand up and down my arm. "Lucy, Lucy," she said. "Oh my dear child."

Then she turned to William and said, "And where were you, young man, while your poor wife was getting molested?"

William shrugged. This is how he was with his mother. Playfully rude.

Catherine bought me clothes. Frequently she bought clothes she liked, but sometimes she let me buy something I liked: a striped shirt to wear with a pair of jeans, a blue-and-white dress with a dropped waist that I loved. Once she wanted to buy me white loafers. "You will live in these," she said. I asked her not to buy them, I would never have worn them; they were something she would have worn, this is what I thought but did not say, and in the end she did not buy them.

She did, a few months after William and I were married, get rid of a coat that I loved. I had bought it in a thrift shop for five dollars and I loved the huge cuffs and the way it swung when I walked, it was navy blue, I just loved that coat, I thought it was *me*. And Catherine threw it away one day after taking me to buy a new one. I don't remember watching her throw it away, I only remember that she laughingly said that she had done so when I asked where it was. "You have that nice new one now," she said.

The funny thing to me, I mean funny-interesting, is that the new coat she bought for me came from a store that was not where they sold especially nice things. I did not know that for a number of years, until I began to sort out the different stores. But it was *almost* a store where people went who had little money. In my youth we had never gone to such a store; we went to almost no stores at all. But my mother-in-law had money; she had it partly because her husband Wilhelm Gerhardt, William's father who became the civil engineer, had left her a very good life-insurance policy, and she got that money when he died. A few years later she got her real estate license and she sold many houses in nice neighborhoods. So she did have money. That is all I am saying here.

She gave me her old nightgowns; they were nice, white with embroidery on them. I wore those.

═

As I contemplated her now, I understood why William, when he had his nighttime terrors of Catherine, would think of me as comfort. It is because—except for our girls who were eight and nine when Catherine died—it is because I am the only person left who had known his mother. Joanne does not count. She moved to the South after they divorced. She never got remarried. I think she never did, I am not sure.

═

Catherine asked me one day early on—William and I were not yet married—to tell her about my family, and I opened my mouth and then tears came down my face, and I said, "I can't." And she stood up from where she had been sitting in a chair and she came and sat next to me on the tangerine couch and put her arms around me and said, "Oh Lucy." She kept saying that, rubbing my arms and my back and pressing my face to her neck. "Oh Lucy."

She said to me that day, "I get depressed too." And I was amazed. No one I ever knew, no grown-up, had ever said that—and she said it sort of casually—and she hugged me again. I have always remembered that. She carried within her that kindness.

Catherine always smelled good; there was a certain perfume and this was her scent. It was because of this that eventually I began to wear a certain perfume—though not hers—and have my own scent. It seemed I could never buy enough body lotion of this scent.

That lovely woman psychiatrist said one day with a shrug, "It's because you think you stink."

She was right.

My sister and my brother and I were told on the playground almost every day at school by the other children, while they ran off with their noses pinched, "Your family stinks."

═

Right before William turned seventy-one, Chrissy told me she was pregnant. I felt a burst of happiness I had not known I could feel again since David had died; William and I spoke on the phone about this—a grandchild!—and he seemed pleased, though not as ecstatic as I was; this is how he is, it is just his nature, is what I mean. But then two weeks later Chrissy had a miscarriage. She called me from home early in the morning, and she screamed, "*Mom!*" She was on her way to the doctor's. So I went immediately to Brooklyn—I took the subway because at that time of day it is the fastest way to get there—and I went to the doctor's office and then I went to her home and we lay on the couch together while she wept; oh, I had not known Chrissy could weep in such a way, and she—taller than I am—lay with her head on my chest until she finally slowed in her crying; her husband was home, he had been at the doctor's office too, but he left us alone in the living room. I did not tell her she would get pregnant again; I did not think that is what she needed to hear. I just held her, and pushed her hair gently away from her face. "Mom," she said, looking at me, "I was going to call her Lucy if it was a girl."

I could not believe it. I said, *"Really?"* And she rubbed her nose and nodded, and said, "Yes, really."

I kept stroking her hair. Then Chrissy said, "You know, I feel so ashamed somehow."

I said, "About what, Chrissy?"

And she said, "Miscarrying. Like why doesn't my body work right?"

"Oh honey," I said. "Honey, millions of women miscarry. It probably means your body *was* working right."

"Huh," she said after a moment, "I didn't think of it that way." She snuggled against me as though she was a small child, and I kept stroking her hair.

Then she finally sat up and said, "I know it's been awful for you having David die."

I said, "Thank you, honey. But don't worry, I'm okay."

Becka came into the apartment then, and she wept as well, which is something Becka does easily, and Chrissy said, laughing, "Okay, stop crying now." I stayed for lunch, and by then I thought Chrissy was doing better, and her husband had lunch with us and Becka too, so I said, "Okay, everyone, I'm going to get going, I love you all," and they said, "Bye, Mom, we love you—" as they always do when we part.

Walking down the sidewalk I thought how my mother had never said I love you to me, and I thought how Chrissy had been going to call the baby Lucy. She *loved* me, my daughter! Even knowing this, I was surprised. In truth, I was amazed.

On the subway home I sat next to a calm-appearing woman with a small child, a little boy. I watched them both; she loved this child. I wondered if she had ever had a miscarriage and, if so, if she had been ashamed. She seemed wonderfully self-contained, only her containment included the boy. He had a small workbook that said Getting Ready for Kindergarten on it, and the woman, I assume she was his mother, was very patiently spelling out *orange, black, red,* as he found the colors inside the book.

That afternoon I called William, and he said that he was afraid he had not responded right when Chrissy had called to tell him earlier. "I told her not to worry, she'd get pregnant again, and she said, Dad, Jesus Christ, is that all you can say? That's what everyone says, and I just lost my child!" And William said to me, "But it wasn't a child yet, why can't she cut me a break?" So I tried to tell William that to Chrissy it had been practically her child. I almost told him that she had been going to call the baby Lucy had it been a girl, but for some reason I did not tell him. And we hung up.

I thought about Chrissy's tears. And Becka's.

When I was a child, our parents would become absolutely furious if my brother or sister or I cried. My parents, my mother especially, would often become furious with us even if we were not crying, but if one of us *did* cry they both became almost insane in their anger toward us. I have written about this before, but I mention it here because a few years ago a woman I know spoke of a nun telling her that she had "the gift of tears." And this is what Becka has as well. And even Chrissy has the gift when she needs it. Crying, for me, has often been difficult. What I mean is I will cry, but I will feel very scared by my crying. William was good about that; when I really cried hard he did not get frightened the way I think David might have; but with David I never cried as I had in my first marriage, not the gasping sobs of a child. But since David has died there are times when I will sit on the floor near my bed—between the bed and the window—and weep with the utter and horrifying urgency of a child. I always worry—living in an apartment building—that someone will hear me. I do not do it often.

═

On William's seventy-first birthday I texted him in the afternoon: Happy Birthday you old thing. And within just a few moments my phone rang. He was calling from work. I said, "How *are* you, William?" And he said, "I don't know." We spoke of the girls briefly—Chrissy seemed to be managing—and then he told me that Estelle had confessed that morning that she had not bought him a birthday present but if there was anything he wanted he should let her know, she had just been too tied up with Bridget and all that was going on with her. So I said, "What's going on with Bridget?" And William said she had some concert at school and that she hated the flute even though Estelle was trying to get her to stick it out one more year, and I felt, as he said this, that I—and maybe he—didn't really know what was going on with Bridget. But I said, "Well, I get it. About the present. You've been married a long time. *Is* there anything you want?" And I was thinking, Oh William, let's make this quick, you are such a baby. This is what I was thinking. Dear God, I was thinking, you are just such a child.

Soon after, we hung up.

═

But there is also this:

Once, after my first book came out so many years ago now, when I was still with William, I had an event to do in Washington, D.C., and I do not remember the event, except that I went down and did it alone—I am sure I was frightened by it as I was by all those things back then—but here is what I want to say: On my way home the weather got bad, there were thundershowers that would not stop and wind and so the airport became increasingly filled with people, and I ended up sitting on the floor next to a young couple from Connecticut. She was pretty and hard and he was nice but reticent. The point is this: As the night went on my fear grew, and I called William from a payphone whenever I could—there was a line for the payphones—and he was trying to help me find a place to spend the night; he called different people he knew in D.C., but no one could do anything, we just had to wait out the weather, and I was really frightened. And then the pretty woman from Connecticut had one of the (at that time) very new cellphones and she brought it out and I watched her call the train station and she and her husband decided they would try and get a train to New York, and I asked if I could go with them, and they said all right. Mostly I wanted to go with them because I was terrified of being alone all night in that vast and packed-with-people airport, and so we went and got a taxi and drove to the train station, and there were just a few seats left and I got on the train, and what I remember is watching New Jersey as the sun came up, and feeling so grateful for my home, so deeply, deeply grateful to be going home to New York, to my home with my husband and my girls. I will never forget it. I loved them all that much—oh desperately I loved them.

So there was that as well.

═

And then the two things happened to William.

The first thing I heard about was on a Saturday in late May. It was the anniversary of David's finding out about his illness, and when William called me I (so stupidly) thought he was calling me about that, and I was surprised and touched that he remembered the exact date. I said, "Oh Pillie, thank you for calling," and he said, "What?" And then I said it was the first-year anniversary of David's illness, and he said, "Oh God, Lucy, I'm sorry," and I said, "No, it's okay, tell me why you called."

And he did say, "Oh Lucy, I'll call back another day. It can wait."

And I said, "Who cares about another day? Tell me now."

So William told me how that morning he had finally gone onto the ancestry website that Estelle had gotten him a subscription for, and then—sounding as though he was having a conversation about a tennis game he had just seen that was interesting—he told me.

This is what he found:

His mother had had a child before he was born. With her husband Clyde Trask, the potato farmer in Maine.

This child was two years older than William, and the website stated her maiden name as Lois Trask and the child Lois had been born in Houlton, Maine, near where Catherine had lived with her first husband, the potato farmer husband Clyde Trask. The birth certificate stated Catherine Cole Trask as her mother and Clyde Trask as her father. Clyde Trask had married someone else when Lois was two years old; there was a marriage certificate for that as well. William could find no death certificate for Lois, only a marriage certificate from 1969, her name was now Lois Bubar—"I looked up how to pronounce it, and it's *boo-bar,*" William said with some sarcasm—and the names of her children, and grandchildren. Her husband had a death certificate from five years ago.

William asked what I thought of that and then said, almost casually, "It's ridiculous, of course, it can't be true. I bet these sites have all kinds of misinformation on them."

I got up and moved to a different chair. I asked him to take me through the steps again; I knew nothing about these websites. So he did, patiently, and as I listened—and I mean this literally—I got chills down my side. "Lucy?" he said.

After a moment I said, "I think it has to be true, William."

"It's not true," he said, firmly. "God, Lucy. Catherine would *never* have left a child, and even if she ever did—which she wouldn't have—she would have spoken to someone about it."

"Why are you so sure?"

"Because that's what these places do—they rope you in, and—"

"What places?" I asked.

And he said, "These dumb-ass websites."

I rolled my eyes, which of course he could not see. "Oh Pill, please, stop it. They don't make up birth certificates. She had a child!"

"I'm going to investigate more," William said calmly.

And he hung up.

I said out loud, "You idiot. Catherine had another kid!" I was astonished. But as I thought about it, it made a kind of weird sense.

═

The year before we married we were most often at William's apartment. I didn't live there, except I kind of did. And we were so happy. I was so happy, and I am quite sure he was too. I would try to cook us meals, although I knew almost nothing about food; I remember he was puzzled by how little I knew about food, but he was very kind about it. And he had a television, which I had never had growing up, and every night we would watch the Johnny Carson show. I had not known such a show existed until then, and every night we watched it sitting together on his couch.

I remember that year that he read to me. It was a children's book, but for grown children, and he had liked it when he was young—it was about a boy who made up a life for himself—and he read me a few pages every night while we lay in bed, and my desire for William would just sit there on top of me. If, when he turned out the light, he did not reach for me—and most nights he did—I would feel a sense of fear and of being bereft. That was how much I wanted him.

We were married at a country club that William's mother was a member of, and it was a very small wedding, some college friends and friends of his mother's, and about an hour before it took place, when I was upstairs getting dressed in a room at the club—my parents and siblings did not attend; in fact they sent nothing and wrote me nothing after I told them about my upcoming wedding—I began to feel a weird sense of something, it is very hard to describe, but it felt a little bit like things were not entirely real, and when I went downstairs and stood next to William and the justice of the peace and we spoke our vows, I almost could not speak. And William looked at me with great love and kindness as though to help me through. But the feeling did not go away.

When we turned around at the end of the wedding, I saw his mother clapping her hands with great joy, and maybe—I am not sure—I missed my mother terribly right then, maybe I had been missing her all along, I do not know. But the feeling I have just described did not go away, and during the little reception afterward I did not feel quite like I was really there. Everything felt a little bit far away, is what I mean, like I was removed from it. And that night in the hotel I did not give myself as freely to my husband as I usually did, the feeling I had was still with me.

The truth is this: That feeling never went away.

Not entirely. I had it my whole marriage with him—it ebbed and flowed—but it was a terrible thing. And I could not describe it to him or even to myself, but it was a private quiet horror that sat beside me often, and at night in bed I could not be quite as I had once been with him, and I tried to not let him know this, but he knew of course, and when I think how I had felt such despair those nights he did not reach for me before we were married, I can understand how he must have felt during our marriage; he must have felt humiliated and bewildered. And there seemed nothing to be done about it. And nothing was done about it. Because I could not speak of it and William became less happy and he closed down in small ways, I could see that happen. And we lived our lives on top of this.

When we first had Chrissy I felt very scared, I had no idea how to take care of a baby and Catherine came and stayed with us for two weeks. "Go, go," she said to us that first week. "You two go out now and have dinner together." In my memory she seemed slightly aggressive as she took charge of the baby—and of us. So we went out to dinner, but I was still frightened, and then William, who had really said remarkably little since the baby had been born, said to me that night, "You know, Lucy, I think I would feel better if she had been a boy."

It was as though something dropped deep inside of me, and I did not say anything about it.

But I have always remembered that. At the time I thought, Well, at least he is being honest.

But we had these surprises and disappointments with each other, is what I mean.

═

I could not stop thinking about Catherine. I am not sure why I knew she had had that child, but I felt certain that she had. I remembered how she'd held Chrissy when Chrissy was a baby; Catherine had taken charge, as I said, during that first visit. But as I thought about this, I sort of remembered other times—later on—when Catherine had a certain fear in her face as she held Chrissy. It is easy to recall this now, but in my memory it is true. And with Becka she was loving but also sometimes oddly distant. Imagine what she was thinking as she held our two little baby girls!

I remembered how she talked very little of her past, very *very* little; she had had an older brother that she always dismissed with a shake of her head, saying, "Oh he had troubles," and the brother had died in an accident at a train crossing years ago. But when Catherine spoke of her potato farmer husband she always put him down, saying that he was "unpleasant" and that they had never loved each other. She had been eighteen when she married him; she did not go to college until she moved to Massachusetts with the German POW, William's father.

About meeting Wilhelm, as William's father was named (although when he came to America for good he too was William), we knew that story well. Wilhelm had been one of twelve prisoners of war who worked on the farm; they were driven in a truck daily from their barracks out near the local airport in Houlton. And Catherine took them doughnuts she had made one day about a month after the men had first arrived, she took them doughnuts to eat with their lunch out by the potato house; she told us the men were not fed enough, and she said that Wilhelm had glanced at her in a way that made her positively shiver.

But here is when Catherine fell desperately—oh just desperately—in love with Wilhelm. The potato farmer, Clyde Trask, had a piano in his living room; his mother had apparently played it, and she had died right before Catherine married Clyde Trask. The piano sat there, it was an old upright. And Catherine said that one day when her husband was not home—he had gone to Augusta because he was in the state legislature and they had some committee meeting even though the legislature was not in session—Wilhelm walked into the house. Catherine was frightened, but he smiled at her; he had a cap on his head and he took it off, and then he walked into the living room and he sat down at the piano and he played.

This is when Catherine fell for him frantically, irretrievably. She said she had never heard anything as beautiful as what Wilhelm played that day; it was summer and a window was partly open, and a breeze picked up the curtain and tossed it gently, and he sat there and played that piano. It was Brahms he played, she found this out later. He played and played, glancing up at her only once or twice. And then he stood up and gave her a tiny bow—he was a tall man with dark blond hair—and he walked past her back out to the fields. She watched him through the window, he had strong arms that showed because his shirtsleeves were rolled up, and on the back of the shirt were the large black letters POW, and he wore the old pants that the POWs wore, and he had boots on and she watched the back of him as he walked to the fields, a tall man walking erect, and he turned around once, just briefly, and smiled, although she was certain that he could not see her watching him from that distance as she stood near the curtains at the window.

Whenever Catherine told us this story, her eyes got very faraway; you could tell that she was picturing this: the man who had stepped into her house and taken his cap off and sat down at the piano and played. "And that was that," she said, returning to us. "That was that."

How they conducted their love affair I do not know, she never said. But apparently Wilhelm knew a little English; that was unusual, Catherine indicated to us, for most of the POWs. But she told us about the day she left her potato farmer husband. It was a year after she had last seen Wilhelm, he had been sent back when the war was over; he had been sent first to England to do reparations—he had to help clean up the war damages there—for six months, and then he returned to Germany. They wrote letters. I do not know if her potato farmer husband found the letters, but she did tell me once that she would walk to the post office every day to see if there was a letter from Wilhelm, and that the postmaster in that small post office in Maine grew suspicious of her; she said that. And she said that the last letter she wrote—after Wilhelm had written her that he was now in Massachusetts—telling him that she would be on the train that pulled into North Station in Boston at five o'clock in the morning, she must have named the day; it was November and there was almost a foot of snow on the ground—that when she went to mail it, she was afraid the postmaster would not send it. Except that he had to, she thought, and he obviously did. She told us that she had waited until her husband's sister came to visit before she left; she wanted the potato farmer husband to not be alone when he realized she had gone. I was always struck with that.

Otherwise I knew almost nothing about Catherine. She would shake her head when I asked her what her childhood had been like. "Oh, not so great," she said one time. "But fine." She never returned to Maine again.

═

I waited a week and then I called William at work and he sounded distracted. I said, "What more have you learned?" And he said, "Oh Lucy, it's just crap. There is nothing more to learn." I asked him what Estelle had said, and he hesitated and then said, "About what?"

"About your mother having another kid," I said, and he said, "Lucy, we don't know that she had another kid," and I still asked him what Estelle had said, and after a moment he said, "She understands it didn't happen."

When we hung up, I realized that William was lying. About what, I was not sure. But there was in his voice something dishonest, is what I thought I heard. I decided I would not call him again about any of it.

Oh I missed David! I missed him dreadfully. Unbelievably I missed him. I thought how he knew I loved tulips, and how he always—always—brought tulips to the apartment; even when they were out of season he would go to a florist nearby and bring me home tulips.

═

When I was a young child, if I or my sister or my brother told a lie, or even if we had not but our parents thought we had told a lie, we had our mouths washed out with soap. This is not at all the worst thing that happened to us in that house, and that is why I will mention it here. We would have to lie down on our backs on the floor of the small living room, and whoever it was that had told the lie—let's say for this example it was my sister, Vicky—then the other two kids, my brother and I, one of us was instructed to hold down her arms, and the other of us held down her legs. And then my mother would go into the kitchen and get the dishcloth and then she would go into the bathroom and scrub the dishcloth with the cake of soap and Vicky would have to stick her tongue out and my mother would shove the rag in and keep moving it until Vicky gagged.

As I have gotten older I think that it was unconsciously brilliant of my parents to involve the other kids in this activity; it kept us apart, as all the things that happened in that house kept us apart.

When it was my turn to lie on the floor I never struggled as my poor brother—who was always terrified at such moments—and my poor sister—who was always furious at such moments—did. I lay there and closed my eyes.

═

Please try to understand this:

I have always thought that if there was a big corkboard and on that board was a pin for every person who ever lived, there would be no pin for me.

I feel invisible, is what I mean. But I mean it in the deepest way. It is very hard to explain. And I cannot explain it except to say—oh, I don't know what to say! Truly, it is as if I do not exist, I guess is the closest thing I can say. I mean I do not exist in the world. It could be as simple as the fact that we had no mirrors in our house when I was growing up except for a very small one high above the bathroom sink. I really do not know what I mean, except to say that on some very fundamental level, I feel invisible in the world.

That couple who let me take the train back to New York with them that night I was stuck in the Washington, D.C., airport: Not too long afterward, they saw my picture in the newspaper and they came to a reading I gave in Connecticut. The woman was all bright smiles; she was really very nice to me, so much nicer than she had been when I was with them in the airport, and it was—I think—because now she thought that I was someone. The night in the airport I had just been a scared person who tagged along behind her. I have always remembered that, how different she was to me the night of my reading. My book had done very well, and the library I read in was packed with people. And I guess she must have been impressed with that.

What she could not possibly have known was that even as I stood before all those people and read and answered questions, I still felt oddly—but very truly—invisible.

For the months of July and August, Estelle and William have always rented a house in Montauk, on the very eastern tip of Long Island.

For a number of years after Catherine died, William and I and the girls would go to Montauk for a week in August; we would stay at a small hotel, and we would walk through the tall grass along a tiny path that led to the beach across the street. We would put large beach towels down and stick an umbrella into the sand. I liked the beach; I *loved* the ocean; I would stare at it and think how it was like Lake Michigan, but not at all. It was the ocean! Though, in truth, I have mixed feelings about our times there.

William very much liked Montauk, but in my memory he was often distant from me there, and from the children as well. One time when the girls were young we had to wait a very long time while William finished a huge bowl of steamed clams in a restaurant. I remember watching him as he peeled the black from the clams' necks and then soaked them in the gray cup of water on the table; he did not speak, and the girls got restless, climbing onto my lap, and then moving around the place, walking close to other tables. "Take the girls outside," he said to me, and so I did. But it still took him forever to finish the clams. I also remember one time when we drove back from Montauk to the city he did not speak to me once.

After our marriage ended I never returned to Montauk.

═

But.

William and Estelle rented a house out there. Bridget went to camp in western Massachusetts; she apparently loved it, and William would come into the city just a few days a week to work in his lab. Estelle stayed out in Montauk, and they entertained a lot there on the weekends. Mostly I know this because Chrissy and Becka would go there and stay a few days, sometimes separately and sometimes together. Becka described the house as having a lot of big windows, and Chrissy said the people they entertained were "terrific bores. From the theater, I guess," is what she said. But Chrissy is a lawyer with the American Civil Liberties Union, and married to the man in finance. Both girls told me how much Estelle cooked, and it made me feel tired to hear that; I have never liked to cook.

═

The second thing that happened to William is this:

On a day in early July, it was a Thursday, William called and said, "Lucy? Can you come over?"

"Over where?" I asked.

"To my apartment."

"I thought you were in Montauk," I said. "Are you okay?"

"Come over right now. Can you? Please?"

So I left my apartment—it was a very hot day, the kind of day when moving about New York is not easy, the heat was so thick—and I got into a cab and went to William's place on Riverside Drive. The doorman said to me, "Go right up, he's waiting for you."

In the elevator I felt very worried; I had been worried since William called me, but the doorman made me even more worried. I got off the elevator and went down the hall to their apartment door, and I knocked, and William called out, "It's open," and so I walked in.

William was sitting on the floor in front of the couch; his shirt was rumpled, and even his jeans looked dirty. He had no shoes on, just socks. "Lucy," he said. "Lucy, I can't believe this."

At first I thought the place had been burglarized because there was a sense of much of it missing.

But this is what had happened:

William had gone to a conference in San Francisco and delivered a paper. He felt at the time that the paper was slight, and he thought people in the audience knew that; he got very little feedback on it. At a reception afterward, men and women he had known for years were gracious to him, but only one man mentioned his paper, and even then William felt it was merely out of politeness. On the flight home he thought about this: that his career was essentially over.

As he stepped into the entranceway of his building—it was midafternoon on Saturday—the doorman seemed extremely serious as he looked at William. The doorman nodded and said, "Hello, Mr. Gerhardt." William did notice that. But William only said, "Good afternoon." He did not know the names of all the doormen though he had lived in the building for almost fifteen years; this particular doorman was one whose name William could not remember. And then, when William unlocked the door of his apartment, he saw immediately that it was different, it seemed more vast, and at first he thought (just as I had when I entered it) that it had been burglarized. On the floor—he almost stepped on it—was a handwritten note from Estelle on a regular-size piece of paper. William handed me the note from where he sat on the floor, and he said, "Keep it." I sat down on the couch and read it. The note said (I did keep it):

Honey, I am so sorry to do this in such a way! I am really sorry, honey.

But I've moved out—I'm in Montauk at the moment

but I have an apartment in the Village. You can see Bridget anytime you want to. Don't worry about any alimony for me, I'm all set. I'm really sorry, William. I am not blaming you for this (but you ARE kind of unreachable a lot). But you're a good man. You just seem faraway at times. I mean a lot of times. I'm really sorry not to have let you know, I guess I am a wimp.

Love, Estelle

I sat there on the couch and said nothing for a long time, just looked around at the apartment. I could not tell what was missing, but there was a hollowness to the place, and the sunlight that came through the window made it feel even more ghastly. Finally I realized that the big maroon chair was gone. And then I saw on the mantelpiece a large vase, and William followed my gaze and said, "Yeah, my Christmas present to her, she left it here."

"God," I said. We said nothing for many more moments. All of a sudden I realized that the rugs were gone except for a small one in the far corner of the room; this is partly why the place looked so bleak. "Wait," I said. "She took the rugs?"

William only nodded.

"God," I said again, quietly. "My God."

Then William said—he was sitting with his long legs out

in front of him; his socks looked dirty and his feet were pointed outward—"Lucy, what scares me is the feeling of unreality I've had. It's been five days and I just can't shake the feeling that this isn't real. But it is. And it scares me. I mean the sense of unreality scares me." Then he said, "Go look in the bedrooms. All of Estelle's clothes are gone, and most of Bridget's, and Bridget's furniture is all cleaned out. And the kitchen has only half the stuff left." He turned his head to look up at me, and his eyes seemed almost dead.

He told me that he had felt waves of exhaustion these five days. He'd slept without dreaming, and he often slept twelve hours, rising only to go to the bathroom, and the fog of his fatigue would descend again. He said, "I never, ever saw this coming."

I touched his shoulder. "Oh Pillie," I said quietly. I looked around again. The vase was glass with colored glass shapes in it. "Oh dear God," I said.

After many minutes, William turned and crossed his arms on my lap where I still sat on the couch and then put his head on his arms. I thought: I could die from this. I touched his head of full white hair.

"Is it true that I'm unreachable a lot?" He looked up from eyes that seemed smaller and were now red. "Do you think that's true, Lucy?"

"I have no idea if you are any more unreachable than the

rest of us," I said, because it was the nicest thing I knew to say.

William got up and sat next to me on the couch. "If *you* don't know, then who does?" He said this with what I thought was an attempt at humor.

"Nobody," I said.

And he said, "Oh Lucy," and he reached for my hand and we sat on the couch holding hands. Every so often he shook his head and whispered, "Jesus."

Finally I said, "You have the money, Pill. Don't stay here. Go to a nice hotel until you get this sorted out."

And it was funny, but he said, "No, I don't want to go to a hotel. This is my home."

I say it was funny, because he called it his home. Of course it was his home. The man had lived here for years. He had eaten countless meals at those wooden tables with his family, he had showered here, read the news, watched television here. But I have still never felt that I had a home. Ever. Except for the one with William years and years ago. I have told you that before.

I stayed there for the afternoon. I went—because he asked me again to do so—and looked into his bedroom and also Bridget's, and everything he had said was true. The blue quilt was a mess on their bed; she had not taken the quilt.

There were dust bunnies on the floor of Bridget's room, I suppose from beneath her bed, which had been taken. "Where is Bridget going to sleep when she comes over?" I asked William when I came back into the living room, and he looked surprised and said, "I haven't thought of that. I guess I'll have to get her another bed."

"And a bureau," I said. Then I said, "Go take a shower and let's go out to eat."

So he did that, and he looked better as he stepped back into the living room in a different—a clean—shirt, rubbing a towel over his white head of hair.

═

We spoke of many things that night at dinner. The restaurant was an old, comfortable-seeming place, and at that time of year we easily got a table and we sat toward the back, and we talked. But I felt terrible. I felt terrible for this man who used to be my husband. We talked a long time about Estelle and Bridget, and then a little bit about our girls; he asked that he be the one to tell Chrissy and Becka about Estelle leaving, and I said, Of course.

Then William said, holding a piece of bread, "Catherine had a kid before me," and I said, "I know that."

William told me how he had researched it—before this conference—and realized his mother must have become pregnant a few months after his father went to England and then to Germany. "So the kid," William had done the math, had all the dates, "would have been about a year old. She would have been practically walking, Lucy, when my mother just strolled right out the door." He looked at me then, and the pain on his face was estimable. It broke my heart, and somewhere I faintly understood that he must have felt that his mother had betrayed him as two of his wives had done.

He added, "But the father, Clyde Trask, he got married a year later to a woman named Marilyn Smith." William spoke the word "Smith" with disdain. "And he stayed married to her for fifty years. They had some boys together."

I reached and squeezed his hand. I said, "Pillie, we're going to get this all figured out. We're going to deal with everything, don't you worry."

He said, "Well, you deal with things, that's for sure."

I said, "Are you kidding? I don't deal with anything!"

And he said, "Lucy. You deal with *everything*."

═

In the taxi on the way back to my apartment that night I thought how I had left William in a similar way, only with more warning. And I had not taken anything except for some of my clothes. But I had told him I wanted to move out. I had told him that I had an image of myself as a bird, folded up in a box, living with him. He could not understand that, and I do not blame him. I got a small apartment just a few blocks away from the brownstone we lived in in Brooklyn then. But I did not move out for almost a year, and then when he was at work one day—it was a Monday and I picked up the phone and I called a mattress store and within two hours a mattress had been delivered to my tiny apartment, and I thought: Oh God, Lucy. Or maybe I didn't think anything. I was just terrified. So I put a bunch of things in a garbage bag and I walked the garbage bag over, and I bought one pan at a drugstore and also one fork and one plate. And I called William and I told him I had moved out.

I always remember his voice that day. He said, "You have?" His voice was so small. "You've moved out?"

It was good of him, I thought in the taxi, not to remind me of this today.

I also thought about Estelle, and I thought—I assumed this—that she could not have done this if she was not involved with another man. I had not mentioned that to William. I wondered who he was, if he was the theater fellow she had said to that night in the kitchen, "Are you bored to death?" It made me angry to think of her. Jesus, I thought,

I can't stand you. She had hurt William, and I couldn't stand her for that.

About Catherine, I did not think a great deal right then. I was more concerned with that empty apartment that William was inside right now. Although in my distress for him, some kind of unpleasantness I felt toward Catherine emerged as well.

═

The night I found out about William's affairs—he had been having more than one—our girls were in bed, they were teenagers by then, and it was around midnight, and he finally told me, in small bits of information and then larger ones. Two days earlier I had found a credit card receipt that I had taken from his pocket to prepare the shirt for the cleaners; it had been for a dinner for apparently two people—this is what the price seemed like to me—at a restaurant in the Village, and he had told me that he was working late that night. I was scared as I showed him the receipt and asked him about it. When he saw the receipt he (I thought) seemed taken aback, but he said that a woman he worked with was having trouble so he had had dinner with her. Why hadn't he told me? I cannot now remember what he said, but it was reassuring and it had assuaged me—sort of. (For a few years at that point I had had dreams that he was cheating on me, and every time I told him William would speak to me kindly and say, “I have no idea why you would be dreaming that.”) But that evening we had had friends over and the woman of the couple went up on the roof with me to have her cigarette and she told me she had been having an affair with a man in Los Angeles. “The sex is great,” she said, inhaling. “The sex is amazing.”

And when she said that to me I knew. About William. I don’t know why, but that was the moment I knew, and when we came downstairs I looked at William and I believe he saw in my look that I knew, and we waited for the guests to leave and then the girls to go to bed, and I told him what the woman had said, and after a while he confessed. First to one, and then to a couple of others. There was a woman that William worked with that he seemed to care for especially, although he said he was not in love with any of them. But he did not tell me about Joanne for another three months. And when he told me about Joanne I thought I might die. I had already thought I would die hearing about the other women. But this woman, Joanne, had been in our house countless times, she had brought the girls to see me in the hospital one summer when I was sick, she had been a friend of mine as well as my husband’s.

—

A tulip stem inside me snapped. This is what I felt.

It has stayed snapped, it never grew back.

I began to write more truthfully after that.

═

"Mom," said Becka into my phone—I was walking down the street to the drugstore the day after having seen William in his apartment—"Mom, what the *fuck*?" So I knew he had told her about Estelle.

"I know," I said. I walked over to a bench on the sidewalk and sat down.

"What the *fuck*?" Becka said again. "Mom, that poor man! Mom!"

"I know, honey," I said. I watched through my sunglasses people going past me, but I did not really see them. Then my phone buzzed and it was Chrissy calling. "Chrissy's calling," I said to Becka, "hold on a minute." Then I pushed the green circle and Chrissy said to me, "Mom, I can't believe this! I just can't believe it!"

"I know," I said.

It was like that, the girls went back and forth with me about the outrage against their father, and I was calm and spoke to them both, and when they both asked me "Is he going to be okay?" I said he would most certainly be okay. I emphasized this, because I did not know myself—except what choice did he have, what choice do most of us have, except to be okay? I said, "He's still reasonably young, and he's very healthy, and he's going to be fine."

Within a week Chrissy had ordered a bed and a bureau for Bridget and she also bought new rugs. "They're much prettier," she said. "They really lighten the place up." She's a wonderful person, Chrissy. She has always taken charge.

In three more weeks, Chrissy called and said, "Mom, we're going to have dinner with Dad at his place. We'd like it if you came."

═

I think I have to mention this, although I have said I would not talk about David, but I think you should know:

When I say I had no home except for William, this is true. David—I told you this before—had been a Hasidic Jew growing up poor right outside of Chicago. But he had left that community at the age of nineteen and he had been ostracized and he had no contact with his family until almost forty years later when his sister got in touch with him. What you need to know is that he and I had this in common: We had, neither one of us, been raised with the outside culture of the world. Neither of us had grown up with a television in the house. We had only a vague knowledge of the Vietnam War, until we taught it to ourselves later on; we had never learned—because we had never heard—the popular songs of the time we grew up in, we had not seen movies until we were older, we did not know the idioms that were used in common language. It is hard to describe what it is like when one is raised in such isolation from the outside world. So we became each other's home. But we—both of us felt this way—we felt that we were perched like birds on a telephone wire in New York City.

But let me just say one more thing about this man—!

He was a short man, and a childhood accident had left him with one hip higher than the other and so he walked slowly and with a severe limp. And he was—being not tall—slightly overweight. What I mean is that he looked as different from William—almost—as a person could look. And I had none of the reaction I had when I had married William. I mean that David's body was always a tremendous comfort to me. David was a tremendous comfort to me. *God,* was that man a comfort to me.

═

When I walked into William's apartment that night to have dinner with the girls and him, I was surprised that the girls' husbands were not there, and I said so, and Becka said, smiling, "We left them home."

It was true that the place looked a great deal better, and I walked through it and exclaimed on everything Chrissy had done. (The vase on the mantel was gone.) And William looked better, though when he bent to kiss my cheek he gave a sigh and squeezed my arm, and I understood it to mean he was doing this for the girls, so they could see that he was all right. The girls both cooked, and the four of us sat in the kitchen—Estelle had left behind the round kitchen table—and William had two glasses of red wine, which he almost never had—I mean, William almost never drank is what I mean. And there was this:

It was unbelievably easy for me to be there. I think we all felt that. It was like a moment out of time, and the four of us were thrust back into the old rhythms that we had had when we were a family; I felt absolutely relaxed, is part of what I am saying. And the three of them seemed that way too. It was remarkable how easy it was for us. I looked at all three of them, and their faces seemed shiny with a kind of happiness.

We spoke of old friends that we had known as a family, we spoke of how Becka had dyed strips of the front of her hair purple for a year when she was a teenager. We told the story, as we had so many times, of how Chrissy, sitting in her car seat one day in the summer—she was three years old—listened to her father, who had pulled the car over because she would not stop fussing, and he had pointed a finger at her and said, "Now you listen to me, you are starting to piss me off," and then Chrissy leaned forward and she said to her father, "No, you listen to me. You are starting to piss *me* off." We all loved that story, and I added, as I always had when it was told, "Your father looked at me, and I looked at him, and then he just started to drive again. We knew who had the power after that." Chrissy, so grown-up now, seemed to blush with the pleasure of this. We spoke of how when they were little we had taken them to Disney World in Florida and Chrissy choked with laughter as she remembered how scared Becka had been at Captain Hook when during the parade he'd stopped and thrust his sword at her. "I was not," Becka said, and we all told her yes, she was. "You were nine years old," Chrissy said, "and you acted like you were three!" And Becka laughed, tears coming into her eyes.

"She was eight," William corrected Chrissy. "She was eight years old."

We stayed in the kitchen, and we laughed and we were happy. Then Becka glanced at the time and she said, "Oh, I have to go—"—her face falling with sudden sadness—and then Chrissy said she had to go too; I glanced at William, and he looked at me and he said, "You go too, Lucy. Now." He stood up. "All of you, out, I'll clean up. Go." And he smiled in a way that made me feel he knew he would be okay and I think the girls felt that as well, and so as we started out of the kitchen Becka suddenly turned and said, "Family hug?" And William and I glanced at each other briefly, a little bit I think like we had been stabbed, because when the girls were very little we would sometimes say "Family hug?" and the four of us would squeeze together in a hug. And we did that now, only the girls were grown, and Chrissy is taller than I am, but we all hugged and then I turned and said, "Okay, everyone, come on," and we went then, the three of us down in the elevator, and when we got to the street Becka had tears seeping from her eyes, and I put my arm around her, and she began to really cry for a minute, and Chrissy looked serious, and then I said, "Take that cab right there, girls, go—"

And then when I got into my own cab a few minutes later I began to cry. The cabdriver said, "Are you okay?" And I told him no, I had lost my husband.

"So sorry," he said, shaking his head. "So very sorry," he said.

==

There is this about my own mother:

I have written about her and I really do not care to write anything else about her. But I understand one might need to know a few things for this story. The few things would be this: I have no memory of my mother ever touching any of her children except in violence. I do not remember that she ever said, I love you, Lucy. When I took William to meet my parents she took me outside right away and said, "Get that man out of here, he is upsetting your father!" And so we left. It had to do, she said, with the fact that William was German, and apparently to my father's eyes William looked German, and it brought back to him many memories of the war and how bad it had been for him. So William and I got into William's car and we drove away.

That day, as we drove, I told William about a few of the things that had happened to me in that tiny house—and earlier in the garage, which William did not know about until that day—and he stayed silent and just kept looking at the road ahead of him. Over the next few years I told him more; he is the only person who has ever known about everything that went on in that tiny house, and the garage before that, that I was raised in.

My mother—because William paid for her to come—came to New York City a number of years later when I was in the hospital for an appendectomy that had made me sicker than it should have and she stayed with me for five nights and it was extraordinary that she did that. It was unbelievable. It made me understand that she loved me. But she never, before the visit or after the visit, would accept a collect telephone call from me, which I sometimes tried to do when I missed her. She would tell the operator, "That girl has money now and she can spend it." But I did not have money then, we were young and just starting out and William only had a postdoctoral.

This does not matter.

What matters is that I went to see my mother a few years after she had come to see me, she was dying in a hospital in Chicago, and I went to see her and she asked me to leave. So I left.

For a long—very long—time, I have believed that she loved me. But when my husband was ill, and then after he died, I have wondered if she did. I think this was because my love with David was so very present. And so I have grown somewhat constricted in my heart about my mother—at times.

My brother lives alone in the house we grew up in. My sister lives in a town nearby, and she and my brother and I met once not so many years ago, and we all agreed that my mother had not been quite right.

I speak to my siblings once a week on the telephone. But for many years we never spoke at all.

—

I tell myself my mother loved me. I think she did in whatever way was possible for her. As that lovely woman psychiatrist said once, "The Wish never dies."

═

Catherine had taken up golf at the country club she joined after William's father died. She played with the same group of women each week. And she taught William how to play golf, although when I met him at college he did not play golf, I mean I never saw him or heard him talk about playing golf. But when we moved back East he played golf with his mother, and the first time they went to play I thought it was like tennis and they would be back in an hour or two. They arrived back more than five hours later and I was so angry—where had they been? And they kind of laughed and said, Lucy, that's how long golf takes.

That year—right before we got married—Catherine arranged for me to have a golf lesson. She took me to a shop at the country club and bought me a golf skirt, it was short and reddish, and she bought me golf shoes, and I felt so strange, I really felt so strange. And then the "pro," as he was called, gave me a lesson, and I wanted to cry, I couldn't stand it that much. But I kept trying to swing and I did not do too well, and when Catherine showed up to get me I think she must have seen my distress. Because I overheard her whisper to William when we went into the club to have lunch, "I think this has all been too much for her."

My birthday was soon after, and Catherine asked me what I would like. I said I would like a gift certificate to a bookstore. The idea of going into a bookstore and *buying* a few books was unbelievably exciting for me. On my birthday she took me out to the garage and showed me a thing with golf clubs in it. Her face shone with light. "Happy birthday," she said, clapping her hands together. "Your own golf set."

I never once played golf.

But Estelle played golf; she and William played golf together in Montauk and also out in Larchmont, where Estelle's mother lived. And even Joanne played, I remembered this as I sat watching the river a few days after we had all had dinner at William's.

═

I checked on William about a week later and he said, "I'm okay," and he said that Bridget had come to stay a few nights, and we hung up. I thought: Okay, I will not call him again; he had been slightly dismissive of me, I felt.

But a few weeks after that—it was almost the end of August by then—he called at night and he said that he was thinking about this woman, Lois Bubar, his half-sister, and whether or not he should contact her. So we talked about that; he said he wanted to reach out to her because time was running out and they were related to each other, but he didn't want to because what if she hated him? She would certainly hate his mother. "I don't know what to do, Lucy," he said. Then he said, "Do the girls know about this?"

And I said, "I never told them, did you?"

And he said, "No, I just figured you would."

And I said, "Well, I thought it was your thing to tell."

"Okay," he said.

He hung up.

Five minutes later he called back, and he said, "Lucy, will you go to Maine with me?"

I was surprised; I didn't say anything.

"Come on," William said. "Let's just go up to Maine for a few days—next week. Let's just do that, Lucy. We'll go up and see what it looks like where this happened. I have the address of where Lois Bubar lives now, let's just go *look*."

"Just look?" I asked. "I'm not sure I understand."

"I don't either," William said.

═

There is this about trips:

Catherine is the one who took us on vacations. I mean where people sit in the sun around the pool on a Caribbean island. The first trip she took us on, we had just been married. Catherine organized everything; the three of us went to the Cayman Islands. I had only been on one airplane before, and that was when William flew me East my senior year in college. I could not believe that I was sitting in the sky, and I had to act nonchalant about it, and I tried to. But it was astonishing.

At least for the trip to the Cayman Islands I had that one plane ride already behind me so I could act natural, or feel sort of natural. But as soon as we got off the plane and stepped out into the blinding sunshine and then took a van to the hotel, I felt quietly horrible. I had no idea—*no idea at all*—what to do: how to use the hotel key, what to wear to the pool, how to sit by the pool (I had never learned to swim). And everyone there seemed so sophisticated to me, everyone else knew exactly what they were doing; dear God, I was petrified! Bodies were splayed about in the lounge chairs, slathered with greasy stuff that made their skin shine in the sun. Someone's hand would go up and a ponytailed waitress would appear in shorts and take their drink order; how did they *all* know what to do? I feel invisible—as I have said—and yet in that situation I had the strangest sensation of both being invisible and yet having a spotlight on my head that said: This young woman knows nothing. Because I did know nothing. And William and his mother pulled up lounge chairs together and sat in them facing the wide ocean before William turned to see where I was, and he waved his arm for me to go over to them. "Lucy," said Catherine, "what's the matter?" She had a canvas hat on with a wide brim. Her sunglasses were directed at me. I said, "Nothing." I said I would be back out soon, and I went to our room—though I got lost and was on the wrong part of the floor for a while—and when I got into our room I cried and cried. And I don't think either of them ever knew this.

Except when I went back out to them as they were lying in their lounge chairs, Catherine was very kind to me, and she took my hand, and she said, "I think this is too much for you."

Catherine's room was next to ours, and each room had a sliding glass door that opened onto a little patio, and the furniture was a light beige and the walls were white. From our room I could hear Catherine going in or out to her patio; I could hear the sliding glass door. At night I begged William to be quiet when we made love; it alarmed me to think of his mother right there. In that tiny house I grew up in I had heard my parents' sexual noises almost nightly, and they were horrifying, appalling high-pitched sounds my father made. I slept very badly that week in the Cayman Islands.

Once the girls were born, I would watch them by the pool, and Catherine would sit next to William and they talked. One time I said to Catherine, "When you were young, did you go on trips like these?" She was reading a magazine and she put it down on her chest and looked straight ahead at the ocean. "No, never," she said. She picked her magazine back up.

I always hated those trips. I hated every one of them.

One time—we may have been married for five years or so—we took a trip at Thanksgiving to Puerto Rico and we stayed at a place much fancier than the hotel on Grand Cayman, with lots of green grass around it and a huge swimming pool, and then the ocean out in front. Maybe because it was Thanksgiving, I don't know why, but I missed my parents awfully, I even missed my brother and sister. And I collected quarters—I went to the man at the front desk and got as many as I could without telling William or Catherine—and I made a phone call by the long bank of payphones; they were lined up in an area of the lobby that was sort of private, and there was mahogany wood behind all these payphones. And I called home, and my father answered. He sounded very surprised to hear me, and I did not blame him; I very seldom called my parents. He said, "Your mother's not home," and I said, "That's okay, Daddy, don't hang up."

And he said, nicely, "Are you okay, Lucy?"

And I said, I blurted it out, I said, "Daddy, we're in Puerto Rico with William's mother and I don't know what to do! I don't know what to *do* in a place like this!"

And my father, after a moment, said, "Is it pretty there, Lucy?"

I said, "I guess so."

And he said, "I don't know what you do, either. Maybe you can just enjoy the scenery?"

He said that to me, that day. My father.

But I could not enjoy the scenery. I was too overwhelmed by watching the girls in the pool; they were so tiny and yet loved to splash in it, and Catherine had bought them blow-up rings that went around them and helped keep them afloat. Once in a while Catherine would get into the pool with the girls, and she would point to me where I stood nearby and say to the girls, "Swim to Mommy, swim to Mommy!" And she would laugh and clap her hands. And then she would get out of the pool and go back to the beach and read. If William was near the pool or, better yet, in the pool, I felt better, I felt safer from all the people who were sitting around the edge, wrists draping over their lounge chairs, eyes closed to the sun. But William would never stay in the pool very long, and I was left there alone with the girls—and I would be frightened.

On the trips back home the girls would be cranky, and (in my memory) their father would be silent as we waited at the airport. Once on the plane I would sit between the girls and try to keep them entertained, although I often felt angry. Because if one of them cried, other passengers looked over with scowls, and William and his mother would be seated somewhere else on the plane.

Since that time I have traveled the world with my work—my books come out and foreign publishers invite me and there are festivals in all parts of the world—and since that time I have traveled to so many places, and I have traveled first-class, where they give you the little kit of toothpaste and a toothbrush and a mask to put over your eyes—I have done all that so many times now.

What a strange thing life is.

═

I met Becka and Chrissy at Bloomingdale's on Saturday; this is something we have done with frequency over the years. We go to the place on the seventh floor where they serve frozen yogurt and then we walk through the store in a desultory fashion. I have written before about doing that with my girls.

But I mention it now because when they showed up Becka said, "Mom! What kind of *crap* is Dad going through? His wife leaves him and he just found out that he has some half-sister? *Mom!*" She stared at me with her brown eyes.

"I know," I said.

Chrissy stood there, looking serious. She said, "It's kind of awful, Mom."

"Yes, I should say so," I said. And both girls said they were glad I was going with their father to Maine.

I took a close look at Chrissy but she did not seem pregnant to me, and she said nothing about it, until—as we were walking through the shoe section after our frozen yogurt—she said, "I'm going to a specialist, Mom. I'm not getting any younger."

"Okay, good for you," I said, and she slipped her arm through mine.

I know there are cultures in our society where a mother would be very pushy and say, Who is the specialist? Can I go with you? What is going on exactly? But that is not my culture; I come from a Puritan background, both my parents came from Puritan stock—which they were proud of—and we did not talk like that to one another. There was not much talk in my childhood house at all.

But when we parted I kissed the girls as I always do, and as is always true there is pain at my leaving them. A little bit, this time, my heart ached more.

"Good luck! Good luck!" they called out from across the street as they started to go down into the subway. "Stay in touch and let us know! Bye, Mom! *Bye, Mom!*"

═

Because I recently mentioned my father I would like to say something more about the man. He also had terrible post-traumatic stress. He had been in World War II, in Germany, and he had been very, very damaged by it. He never spoke of the war; my mother must have told us that he fought in it, because I was aware of that fact growing up. The way in which his post-traumatic stress (although I did not know that term at the time) manifested itself was an anxiety so great that it seemed to produce sexual urges in him almost constantly. Often he walked around the house—

I am not going to say anything more about this.

But I loved him, my father.

I did.

—

I think I have mentioned the business about my father because as I was packing for Maine, I thought of William's father. He had been fighting on the side of the Nazis, as I have said. (And my father had been fighting against them.) There were letters between William's father and Catherine, and she told us that he said, when he got back to Germany, that he "did not like the things the country had done." But none of those letters are in existence—I mean that when Catherine died, William and I never found those letters—and so I guess we do not know what William's father thought about the war, except for one conversation William remembered having with him when William was about twelve, and his father had said that about Germany—that he did not like what they had done. I thought about this as I packed a summer blouse; why had his father come over to America? Did the man just want to be with Catherine? Or did he want to be American? He had been picked up in a ditch in France by American GIs, and he had thought that they would shoot him, but they did not. And he said—according to William and Catherine—that he wished he could find those men and thank them. He probably did want to be with Catherine, and also to be an American. Probably both. He went to MIT and, as I have said, became a civil engineer.

But I was thinking about William's night terrors: how he said that he pictured the gas chambers and crematoriums.

And I thought how when William came into money from his grandfather who had profited from the war, and Catherine was still alive at that time, she had said very little about it. But she did say to me, lying on the tangerine couch, not long after this had happened, "It's dirty money. He should give it all away."

But William did not give it all away; he became very rich. Although, as I have said, he does give money away. When I had asked William about the money—and what he would do with it—he was always closed off. "I'm keeping it," he said. And he did. I have never understood this, but now I wonder if perhaps he thought something was owed to him. Was this because his father had died when William was so young? I know that people, when they have had a loss, sometimes unconsciously believe that they should then take something in return. But it was many years later that William got this money, although that sense of loss I think is always there. But I do think now there was—and still is—some sense William had that he was owed something.

Catherine and her husband never went together to Germany. And I thought about how neither of them—except when Wilhelm went back to Germany after the war—ever returned to the scenes of their childhood again. They had had that in common.

But it came to me, as I put a nightgown into my suitcase for our trip to Maine, it came to me suddenly that this is what William's life rumbled over, like a train on loose tracks: the images from Dachau that would not leave his brain after he had gone there with me so many years ago. He had been petrified by what he saw there in Germany. He must have been deeply haunted by his father's role in it. Unspeakably frightened. It had unmoored him.

This is what I thought.

Perhaps he felt—if he allowed himself to think about it—that this experience had changed him in some way more than any other, perhaps even more than his mother's death?

And yet it was after his mother's death—I think this, anyway—that he had started with the women, and with Joanne.

I am only saying: I wondered who William was. I have wondered this before. Many times I have wondered this.

═

I should mention:

I never told the girls about their father's affairs. I thought: They will never hear about this from me. And so I never told them, even after I had left William, I still did not tell them about their father's affairs.

And then one day—it was not even that long ago, maybe six or seven years now—we had gone to Bloomingdale's together, the girls and I, and afterward we went for a glass of wine at a restaurant nearby. When we sat down they glanced at each other and then Chrissy said, "Mom, did Dad have an affair when you guys were married?"

For many moments I said nothing, I just watched them watching me with their clear eyes. Then I said, "Are you ready for this conversation?" And they both said yes.

So I said, "Yes, he did."

And Becka said, "With Joanne?"

And I said, "Yes."

And then I said—I wanted to be fair—I said that I had been having an affair when I left their father. I looked from one girl to the other and I said that at that time I had fallen in love with a writer from California and I was having an affair with him. I told them this writer had been married, and then I said, "And he had kids. So I did that. You should know."

They seemed more interested than surprised by this—which surprised me—and Chrissy said, "What happened?" And I said, "Well, his marriage eventually ended, but—Well, I mean, I knew that I wouldn't end up with him, and I didn't. But I knew I couldn't stay with your father after that." What most surprised me about their response was how little they seemed to want to know about this. Chrissy wanted to know more about Joanne. "How long?" she asked, and I said that I did not know.

Becka said, "I used to like her." And Chrissy turned to her and said, "You *loved* her," almost angrily, and I said, "Well, why wouldn't you, I mean you didn't know."

They sat there quietly and then Becka shook her head and said, "I don't understand anything in this life."

I said, "I don't either."

When we parted, the girls kissed me and hugged me and told me they loved me. I was terribly shaken by our conversation, and they did not especially seem to be. This is what it seemed like to me.

But who ever really knows the experience of another?

When William met me at LaGuardia Airport I saw him from afar and I saw that his khakis were too short. A little bit this broke my heart. He wore loafers, and his socks were blue, not a dark blue and not a light blue, and they showed a few inches until his khakis covered them. Oh William, I thought. Oh William!

He looked exhausted; there were darkish circles around his eyes. He said "Hi Button" and sat down next to me. He had with him a small suitcase with wheels, it was dark brown, two-toned. I understood that it was expensive. He looked at my wheelie suitcase, which was a blazing violet color, and he said, "Really?"

"Oh stop," I said. "It never gets lost."

"I should think it wouldn't."

Then he crossed his arms and looked around and said, "You ever been to Maine, Lucy?" A baby was crawling across the carpeted floor with its mother behind it; she was wearing a Snugli on her front and she smiled at us, and I saw William smile back at her.

"Once," I said, and he said, "Yeah?"

"I was invited to that college in Shirley Falls to give a reading. I thought I told you about that."

"Tell me again," he said. His eyes were moving around the place.

"I don't know which book it was, my third? Anyway, the chairman of the English Department invited me up—he was a short-story writer—and I spent the whole afternoon with him, listening about his mother, who was getting old, and all the trouble he was having about that— And as we walked around the campus, I kind of noticed that there were no ads for me that night at all that I could see. So he took me to dinner and then we went to this room with about a hundred chairs set up. And not one person showed up."

William looked at me now. "Seriously?"

"Yeah, absolutely seriously. Only time that ever happened. So we waited about half an hour, then I went off to my room and he emailed me and said he was so sorry, he had no idea why that had happened. And it didn't even occur to me until later that at least *his* students should have shown up. He must not even have told them, I think. I emailed him back not to worry about it."

"Jesus," William said, "what was his problem?"

"I don't know."

"I do." William looked at me with almost anger in his face. "He was jealous of you, Lucy."

"Really?" I said. "I don't know about that."

William sighed and then shook his head slowly, looking again at the baby crawling across the floor. "No, you wouldn't know, Lucy," he said. He tugged on his mustache. "Did they pay you?"

"Oh, sure. I mean I can't remember. You know, something small, I'm sure."

"*Jesus,* Lucy," William said.

═

We arrived in Bangor about fifteen minutes before ten o'clock at night; there had been only a handful of people on the small plane. Walking through the Bangor airport—it was not well lit, and it was kind of eerie—I noticed many signs welcoming veterans home, and William said he had researched this, it had been an old Air Force base, and the runway was very long. It was the place that many people in the armed services overseas first stopped when they came back from wherever they had been. Or left from: It was their final place to leave from in the United States. He said that during the Iraq War this had been the place that so many had come into on their way home, and that the people of Maine had made a point of greeting them. There was a hallway that we did not walk down, but it said in large letters GREETERS HALL. It was almost like a museum in some way. And it made me think of my father. My father had come back from Germany on a ship to New York, and he had taken the train all the way back to Illinois. But was it possible that William's father had gotten to Maine this way; had he been flown in here as a POW?

"No," William said, "he took a train from Boston, after a boat from Europe, I've been reading about this stuff."

There was a strange sense of something surreal.

And then I saw a man who (I think) was going to spend the night at the airport; he was not old or young, and he had with him many large white plastic bags, not suitcases, and he was alone in a section of the airport where the lights were turned down very low. I thought he saw me looking at him; he stopped eating from a big bag of potato chips he had on his lap.

Our hotel was connected to the airport: You walked through a walkway, and the lobby of the hotel—which did not seem like a lobby although there were two chairs—was right there. William checked us in—separate rooms—and I turned and looked at a bar immediately behind us. Men and a few women were seated on tall wooden chairs, all watching the television that hung above them. I stepped away from William and I asked the woman behind the bar if I could please have a glass of chardonnay. "Bar's closed," she said without looking up. "Closes at ten." She was holding glasses under a stream of water from a sink.

"Please?" I asked. The clock on the wall indicated that it was not even five past ten, and the woman didn't say anything more, but she was unpleasant in her manner as she poured my wine.

With my glass of wine in hand, I wheeled my violet suitcase behind William—we were in rooms next to each other—and when I went into my room, it was very cold: The thermostat was set at 60 degrees. All my life I have hated being cold. I turned the air conditioner off, but I knew that the room would stay too cold for me. In the bathroom was a small (tiny) bottle of mouthwash and also, wrapped in cellophane, a man's plastic comb. I kept staring at it: This was exactly the kind of comb my father had had. I had not seen such a comb for years, so small and plastic you could bend it in half and make it snap if you chose to. I knocked on William's door and he let me in and he said, "Jesus." His room was cold as well. He had the television on; he muted it as I came in. I sat on the edge of the bed and saw an advertisement for The History of Button Collecting—there were three different ceramic bowls shown, filled to the top with a variety of buttons, placed on a woven piece of material on a wooden table—and then it was followed by an advertisement for Alzheimer's Aid.

"Tell me the plans for tomorrow," I said.

We would have breakfast on the way and then we would go to Houlton and drive past the house of Lois Bubar. Just to see. She lived at 14 Pleasant Street. Then we might drive to Fort Fairfield, because Lois had been crowned Miss Potato Blossom Queen there in 1961, and William had a photo of her he had found online as she was driven through the streets of Fort Fairfield. I stared at the photo on his iPad, but it was an old photo and I could not see if the woman (she was so young) looked like Catherine or not. But she had been pretty, I could see that. She was on a float, and the float had a great deal of crêpe paper on it, and the streets were packed with people and cars and some buses.

"Then, if we have time, I'd like to go to Presque Isle, because that's where Lois Bubar's husband came from, so we could just take a quick look around."

"Okay," I said. "But why?"

"Just to see it all," William said.

"Okay," I said.

"So we'll take the turnpike to Houlton in the morning and we'll just see what we see," William said. He looked old to me. He was slumped as he stood by the bed, and his eyes were not bright.

"'Night, Lucy," he said when I got up to leave.

I turned and I said, "How are your night terrors these days, William?"

William opened his hand and said, "They're gone." Then he added, "My life got worse, so they stopped."

"I get it," I said. "Good night."

I called the front desk and asked them for an extra blanket and they brought it to me forty-five minutes later.

═

That night I dreamed of Park Avenue Robbie. In the dream he was agitated, and I woke up and went into the bathroom and then got back into bed and I thought about him.

After I left William, now so many years ago, I had a sort-of affair (I am not speaking of the writer I mentioned earlier; this sort-of affair was later) with a man I referred to—with my friends—as Park Avenue Robbie. I had met him at a class at the New School where I was studying World War II to try to understand my father better, to see what I could find out about the Battle of the Bulge and also the Hürtgen Forest, because my father had been at both places during the war, and he had remained a terribly distressed man, as I have said. My father had died the year before I took this class.

I first said hello to Park Avenue Robbie in the elevator, and only later did I realize that in some way—some expression on his face—he reminded me of my father. He was old enough to be my father, although my father had been older. But Park Avenue Robbie was dressed nicely; he was tall and wore a long navy blue coat.

When I first went to his apartment on Park Avenue, I was surprised at how unlived-in it seemed, and in a way it was unlived-in. Park Avenue Robbie had been married twice, and his latest woman friend had left him recently for a fireman—it was the fireman part that Robbie could not seem to get over. "A *fireman,*" he would say, and sometimes laugh, and sometimes just shake his head. "A goddamn fireman. She was just tired of me, I guess," he said of the ex–woman friend.

We went to bed and he was very kind but then he said "I'm shooting into Mommy! I'm shooting into Mommy!" and this frightened me almost beyond reason. After that I had to take two tranquilizers I had in my pocketbook and then I fell asleep next to him and slept through the night with my head near his chest.

Every time he said that.

For three months, we were together on Saturday nights.

═

William rapped on my door in the morning; he was wearing the khakis that were too short and I had the same reaction I'd had when I first saw him wearing them at the airport the day before, but I was tired from my night and I did not feel it as strongly.

Right away William told me—he was standing in the doorway to my room—that when he had gotten into bed the night before he'd had a sensation of holding Becka when she was probably a year old. "Her sweaty—remember how she used to sweat?—her sweaty little face and her head nestled into my neck. Whew, Lucy." He looked at me, and I felt a rush of love for him, for the pain his face showed in remembering our little child.

"Oh Pillie," I said. "I know what you mean. Sometimes I have memories that are sharp like that."

He stared at me, and then I realized he wasn't really seeing me.

"Did you sleep?" I asked him, and he broke into a smile then, his mustache moving, and he said, "I did. How crazy is that? I slept like a baby."

He did not ask about my sleep and I did not tell him.

We pulled our little suitcases behind us down to the car rental place and we got into the car. The day was sunny and warm but not too warm. It seemed like empty parking lots went on forever. On the ride out of the airport we passed by two signs, one on top of the other: Sequel Care on top and Visiting Angel on the bottom—that was the bigger sign, with an angel spreading itself out in yellow and purple. "People are old up here," William told me. "It's the oldest, whitest state in the union."

On the turnpike there were almost no cars in sight. Grass was coming up through the concrete next to the road. We passed a sign that said Speed Limit 75 MPH. As I gazed out of my window I saw the top of a tree whose leaves were orangey-red, and yellow leaves that were changing along the way, and one little bright red tree among all the trees lining the road. The grass by the side of the road was sort of bleached of color; it was very August-looking in the lack of rich green. Beyond it were tall trees.

And then I remembered:

Throughout my marriage to William, I had had the image—and this was true even when Catherine was alive, and more so after she died—so often I had the private image of William and me as Hansel and Gretel, two small kids lost in the woods looking for the breadcrumbs that could lead us home.

This may sound like it contradicts my saying that the only home I ever had was with William, but in my mind they are both true and oddly do not go against each other. I am not sure why this is true, but it is. I suppose because being with Hansel—even if we were lost in the woods—made me feel safe.

As we drove I became aware of a sensation that was familiar, and it had started the night before with the airport seeming so surreal, almost not like an airport at all. What I became aware of was this:

I was scared.

The trees were getting scrubbier, then there was a long stretch of thick pines. In a few more minutes I saw on the left a field of skinny birch trees. But otherwise the wide-open road was endless. There were no signs anywhere. And there were no other cars, except for one or two that passed us by.

I have mentioned earlier how easy it is for me to become frightened, and as we drove up this turnpike with barely another car in sight I thought: Oh I wish I had not come!

I am afraid of things that are not familiar. And New York has been where I have lived for many years, and that is familiar: my apartment, my friends, the doormen, the city buses that sigh at each stop, my daughters. . . . All of that is familiar. And where I was was not familiar, and it frightened me.

It frightened me a great deal.

And I could not tell William, because I suddenly felt that I did not know him well enough to tell him that I was scared.

Mommy, I cried inside myself, *Mommy, I am so frightened!*

And the nice mother I have made up over the years answered: Yes, I know.

We drove and drove, and William was silent, staring through the windshield at this endless road ahead of us. He finally glanced over at me and said, "Okay if we stop for breakfast now?" I nodded. He pulled off at an exit. I was no longer watching things through the window.

In the parking lot, right up near to the front door of the place, we walked past a car that was filled with garbage. Every space of it—except for the driver's seat—was filled with garbage. Trash. Nothing was growing, but there was to the ceiling of the car—the car was an old sedan—trash: newspapers and old wrappings of waxed paper and small cardboard cartons of the sort that food came in. The license plate had a big V on it and also said VETERAN.

—

"William," I murmured, and he said, "What?" I said, "Did you see that?" And he said, "It was hard to miss," as he pulled the door open and stepped inside the restaurant before me, but he said it in a way that was cold—to my ears—and my panic grew.

Oh, to panic!

If you have not been there, you cannot know.

There were maybe ten other people in the place; it was like a log cabin inside—I mean there were round logs that made up the walls—and the waitresses were very nice. A young one with really red lipstick took us to a booth, and she was short and almost plump and very bright in her greeting. William looked at the menu, but I was not hungry and when the waitress came back I ordered one scrambled egg, and William ordered eggs and hash.

Across from us—to the right—was a man with no teeth at all, and he was sitting with two other men, and the one with no teeth was talking about needing a passport.

"William," I said.

He looked at me. "What's the matter?"

I said quietly, "I'm panicking."

And I saw—I felt I saw—William droop inwardly, and he said, "Oh Lucy, why in hell are you panicking."

"I don't know," I said.

"You still get like that?"

"Not for a while," I said. "Not even—" I was going to say not even after my husband died. That grief is different from panic. But I did not say this.

I swear I saw William almost roll his eyes. "What am I supposed to do?" he asked, and I hated him then.

"Nothing," I said.

Then William said, "Probably it reminds you of your childhood up here."

I said, "It does not remind me of my childhood. Have you seen one field of soybeans?" But then I saw that he was right. Until we had stopped at this little place for breakfast we had seen almost no one, and the isolation made me panic.

"Well, Lucy." William sat back. "I don't know what to do for you. As you know, my wife left me only seven weeks ago."

"And my husband died," I said. I thought: Is this a competition?

William said, "I know that. But I don't know what to do for your panic, I have never known what to do for your panic."

And I said, "Well, you could hold the door open for me instead of pushing yourself through it." I added, "And you could wear a pair of pants that were long enough, for another thing. Your khakis are too short and it depresses the hell out of me. Jesus, William, you look like a *dork*."

William sat back; his face broke into real surprise. "Seriously? Are you sure?" He moved himself across the seat and stood up. "Really?" he asked, looking down.

"Yes!" I said, and his mustache moved.

He sat back down across from me, and he threw his head back and laughed one of his real—genuine—laughs that I have not heard in ages.

And my panic left me.

"Listen to you," William said. "Lucy Barton telling someone their pants are too short."

"Well, I *am* telling you. They look ridiculous."

And William laughed more. "Calling me a dork? Who says dork anymore?"

"I do," I said, and William laughed again.

"I just bought these pants recently," he said. He added, "I wondered if they were too short."

"They are. They are too short."

"I didn't have my shoes on when I tried them on."

"Forget it," I said. "But you should give them away."

And I was happy because of William's laughter. Everything was all right after that.

—

The waitress brought us astonishing platters of food. William's plate had a pile of reddish hash and two fried eggs on top of the hash and potatoes over that, and also three thick slices of bread. On my plate was a mess of scrambled eggs and also greasy bacon and the three huge slabs of bread as well. "Oh God," I said, just as William said, "Jesus."

"Okay, now listen. What do we do with Lois Bubar?" William asked. He poked around the reddish stuff on his plate and then put a bite into his mouth.

And I said, "We'll figure it out when we get there."

We talked about Lois, her being Miss Potato Blossom Queen, and whether she could have any idea that her mother had left her. William thought she would know; I was not so sure. "Yeah, who knows, who knows," William said. Then he shook his head. "Oh, man," he said.

Eventually the waitress came over and said she could box up the rest of the food for us to take away. William said, "Oh, that's okay. I think we're through."

"You sure?" asked the waitress. She seemed surprised, and she pursed her red lipsticked lips.

"Yes," William said, and she said she would bring us the check. "Maybe she's a relative of mine," William said. He did not say it jokingly.

"Maybe," I said.

On the way out of the diner, William opened the door and made an exaggerated gesture of ushering me through it.

We drove through the town where the diner was, passing a sign that said Libby's Color Boutique: Carpet, Laminate, Vinyl Flooring CLOSED. As we drove out of the town we saw American flags on many telephone poles, flag after flag, and interspersed with them was an occasional black flag for a POW. We could not find the turnpike entrance for a while. We kept driving through winding roads, and by the side of the road at one point were short little cat-o'-nine-tails, also goldenrod, and a grass that almost had a pinkish tinge to its top but was otherwise brown and dry-looking. There were no other cars, or even people seen, in the middle of a day, a Wednesday in late August. But there were lots of almost-falling-down houses, and lots of stars on the sides of these houses for veterans, gold stars for the ones who were dead.

We passed by signs that said Pray for America. And cabins for United Bible Camp.

A pile of rusted-out junk cars was next to an old building that hadn't, it looked, been used in years and years, all of it standing back from the road.

—

I said, "If I were a man who wanted to kill a young girl and get rid of her body and get away with it, this is where I'd do it and dump her, Jesus."

William glanced over at me. His mustache moved as he smiled, and he put his hand briefly on my knee. "Oh Lucy," he said.

But as soon as I had said that—about if I were a man who wanted to get rid of a young girl's body—I realized this:

That driving down this road and seeing the falling-down houses and the grass by the side of the road and no people around, I had an almost-memory of driving with my father in his truck and me in the passenger seat next to him as a very young child, the window open and my hair blowing in the wind, only the two of us—where would we have been going? But the memory was not one of the dismalness of my childhood. Instead, something in me moved deep, deep down and I felt almost—what can I say that I felt?—but it was almost a feeling of freedom as I rode alongside my father in his old red Chevy truck. As I rode now next to William I almost wanted to say, with a sweep of my hand: These are my people. But they were not. I have never had a feeling of belonging to any group of people. Yet here I was in rural Maine and what had just come to me was an understanding, I think that is the only way I can put it, of these people in their houses, these few houses we passed by. It was an odd thing, but it was real, for a few moments I felt this: that I understood where I was. And even, also, that I loved the people we did not see who inhabited the few houses and who had their trucks in the front of these houses. This is what I almost felt. This is what I felt.

But I did not tell that to William, who came from Newton, Massachusetts, and not the poor town of Amgash, Illinois, as I had, and who had lived in New York City for so many years. I had lived in New York City for years as well, but William inhabited it—his tailored suits—and I felt that I had never inhabited New York as he had. Because I never had.

═

I thought then of a woman I had met at a party. It was the first—and only—party I had gone to since David died, and I had expected it to be ghastly. But a woman was there, she was maybe ten years younger than I am, I would say around fifty-three or so, and she told me how she had gone online to a site called Ijustwanttotalk.com and it had changed her life. She told me this with open-eyed forthrightness—there was a tiny little piece of eye makeup that was caught in the corner of her eye, which I kept wanting to tell her—although I never would have—and then I stopped wanting to tell her that and I just listened, it was fascinating. She had recently come back from a trip to Chicago where she met a man at the Drake Hotel—she said it was their third meeting—and they just talked. That's what they did.

I asked her if she was afraid—I meant meeting a man—her age, she had said—and she said she had been at first, but when she saw him (and she placed her hand on my arm) she thought, Oh he is just so *lonely*! "And so was I," she said, and nodded. She said they took turns talking: She had needed, she said, to talk about her mother-in-law, who had died years earlier, but she felt "unfinished with her," and this fellow, his name was Nick, wanted to talk about his son, who was just never right, and his wife was sick of talking about it, and so when it was his turn to talk this is what he talked about. "And we just listen to each other," she said. She took a sip from her sparkling water—no wine, I noticed—and nodded, and she kept nodding. "I don't even know if his name is really Nick," she said.

I asked if she thought she might fall in love with him.

And she took another sip of her sparkling water and said, "It's funny that you should ask me that, because when I first saw him I thought, Oh my God, no, I could never fall for him! Which was a good thing, of course. But you know, it's funny, because this last time after seeing him, I've just been *thinking* about him, and you know, it might have the tinge of—"

"Hello!" a younger woman said to her then, throwing her arms around her, and the woman I was talking to said, holding up her glass of sparkling water, "Oh my God it's *you*!" And that was the last I saw of her.

People are lonely, is my point here. Many people can't say to those they know well what it is they feel they might want to say.

═

We arrived in Houlton around noontime. The sun was shining down on big brick buildings: a courthouse, a post office. Main Street had a few shops—there was a furniture store and a dress shop—and we drove slowly through and then I saw a sign that said Pleasant Street, and I yelled, "William, we're on Pleasant Street!" I looked out the window and the houses were small and wooden, two white ones we passed. And then we passed by number 14, and it was the nicest house on the block. It was not a small house: It was three stories and freshly painted a dark blue with red trim, and it had a little garden in the front, and a hammock was in the front yard as well. William stared at it as we drove past, and then he kept driving and we pulled over on the next block up.

"Lucy," he said.

And I said, "I know."

We sat there for a few minutes with the sun coming through the windshield, and I looked around and there was a library right near us. "Let's go to the library," I said.

"The library?" William said.

"Yes," I said.

═

Inside the library we saw a staircase that wound its way up and also a checkout counter, and a couple of people were in there, a young woman and an old man, they were both reading newspapers. It had a very nice feel to it, the way a library should feel in a small town. The librarian looked up at us. She was maybe in her mid-fifties, and she had hair that was almost without color, and by that I mean just a very pale brown—she must have been blond in her youth—and her eyes were not big or small, what I mean is she looked very neutral, but she was pleasant and she said to us almost immediately, "Is there anything I can help you with?" So perhaps she knew we were from out of town.

I said, "We're visiting because my husband's father was a German POW who came here to work in the potato fields. Do you have anything on that?"

And she watched us, and then she came around from behind her desk and said, "Yes, we do." She brought us over to a corner of the main room devoted to the German POW experience, and I saw William's face moving with emotion when he saw this. There were pieces of artwork on the wall in that corner that had been painted by some of the German POWs. And there were old magazines opened to articles about the POWs, and also a book that was slender.

"My name is Phyllis," the woman said, and William shook her hand, which I thought seemed to surprise her. She asked his name and he told her and then she turned to me and asked me my name and I murmured, "Lucy Barton." "Well, you have yourselves a look," Phyllis said, and she pulled up two armchairs nearby for us to sit in and we thanked her.

There was a shelf of old photographs, and as I peered at one I said, "William! Here he is!" The photograph gave the names of four men who were shown kneeling on the ground. One was smiling, and the rest were not. Wilhelm Gerhardt was on the end of the group. He was not smiling. His cap was not on straight and he looked at the camera with a serious look, almost a Screw You look, I thought. William took the photograph and kept staring at it; I watched his face as he looked at it. And then I looked away.

When I looked back, William was still gazing at the photograph; he finally turned his face to me and said, "It's him, Lucy." Then he added in a quieter tone, "It's my *father*." I looked again at the photograph, and I was struck—again—with the look on William's father's face. All the men seemed thin, but William's father's brow was dark and his eyes were dark and he seemed to carry within himself a small disdainfulness.

Phyllis was still standing behind us and she said, "We're very proud of how they were treated when they were here. Look at these—" And she showed us in a book copies of a few letters that some POWs had written back to the farmers they had worked for once they had gone home. I saw that each letter was asking for food to be sent over to Germany. "One farmer sent boxes and boxes of supplies to them," Phyllis said, and she flipped through the narrow book and showed us a photo of the farmer loading many large boxes onto a conveyor belt. The farmer's name was not Trask. I had not expected that it would be. "You take your time," Phyllis said, and she walked away, back behind the checkout desk.

═

William nudged me and pointed to one line toward the back of the slim book he was reading. It quoted a POW as saying that on the morning of Hitler's birthday, April 20th, they had sewn swastikas out of purple material and hung them about the barracks. Then I found in one of the letters written after the war that there had been a period of time when the prisoners had not been fed enough. And I thought of Catherine making doughnuts for the men. We sat there for over an hour looking through the materials, and then Phyllis came back and said, "My husband is retired, and he'd like to take you out to the barracks—well, what's left of them—if you care to see where they were. Out by the airport."

William's face shone with appreciation. "Oh, that'd be great," he said. She texted on her cellphone and then said to us, "He'll be here in ten minutes," so we collected our things and went back to the front desk. On the front desk was a pile of my books. "Do you mind signing these for the library?" Phyllis asked. And I said, Of course I will, but I was amazed that she knew who I was (I am invisible as I have said) but I stood there and did that.

Phyllis's husband was a man named Ralph, and he was as pleasant as his wife was. He also had the colorless hair that used to be blond and he wore khakis—the right length—and a red T-shirt, and we went with him in his jeep. As he drove us toward the airport he spoke to William mostly—William was sitting up front and I was in the backseat—and the sun was shining, and he drove us for about fifteen minutes and then showed us the tower that was still standing, a guard tower, it was not very high, and then he drove into a dirt road area and let the car idle for a minute and showed us all that remained of the barracks where, at some points, more than a thousand POWs had lived. There was only a concrete corner left.

A weird thing happened to me then. I am not exactly sure how to make this sound believable, but I will just say what happened:

I looked at the concrete that was left and there were green leaves that came down over it, and the sun shone and made the green leaves glint in the sun, and then I felt a sort of a lurch in my head, and everything that Ralph was saying was something that I knew he would be saying. What I mean is that right before a word came from his mouth, I knew what the word would be. They were not important words, only about how the place had been constructed and what they had used for insulation. Except in my head it was a woman's voice that had already told me exactly what he was telling me. I was really thrown. I thought: Is this déjà vu? And I knew it was not. It was lasting longer than that, and it was a very strange moment. Or many moments.

When Ralph dropped us off back at our car we all shook hands and William and I thanked him, and then we got into the car and I told William what had happened, and he looked at me for a while, his face searching. "I don't get it," he said.

"I don't either."

"But was it like a *vision*?" he asked. I have had a few visions in the past (my mother had visions as well), and even William, a scientist, knew this about me and believed what I had told him.

"No," I said. "It was only what it was." Then I said, "It was a bit like I had slipped between universes for a moment. Only it was longer than a moment."

He seemed to absorb this, and shook his head. "Okay, Lucy," he said, and he started the car.

═

My mother's visions:

A woman who was a client of hers—my mother took in sewing and alterations—was going in for gallbladder surgery, and the night before she went in my mother dreamed that the woman had cancer. The next morning, my mother was weeping by our old washing machine, and I asked, What is wrong?, and she told me this woman was going to be "filled with it"—and the woman was. The woman died ten weeks later.

A man in our town killed himself, and my mother had predicted that he would a few weeks earlier. "I saw it," she said one day. And then he did; he shot himself in a field. He was a deacon of the Congregational church and he was a nice man, I remember him smiling at me when we went to the church on Thanksgivings for their free meal.

A boy went missing when I was very small, and my mother said he had fallen down a well. She said she saw it in a vision. My father told her she should tell the police, and she said, "Are you *crazy*? They'll think I'm crazy! Do we need that?" She said, "Do we need people thinking that in this town?" But then the boy was discovered down the well and she didn't have to tell anyone. Only we knew. He lived.

When Chrissy was born I received a letter from my mother—I had not told her I was pregnant—and she wrote, You have a new baby girl, I had a vision of you holding a baby blanket and I knew it was a girl.

These were things I always accepted about my mother.

My own visions, often enough, did not come true and I dismissed them. (Although I had had my dreams about William's affairs, if those were even visions and I think they were not, really—) But there is this one thing:

Years ago I had taught at a college in Manhattan, and I had a good friend who taught there too, and once I had gone to visit her in her country home on Long Island and I left my watch; it was a dime-store watch, worth almost nothing, and I did not think about it and did not ask her about it. But one morning—many, many months later—as I was getting on the subway I pictured the watch in my mailbox at the college—the mailboxes were just open slots on a wooden frame—and when I got there it was exactly the way I had pictured it, just sitting there in my mailbox. That was the weirdest vision I've had. I mean because it meant nothing to me. But there it was.

═

We tried to have lunch in Houlton, but the one place we found closed at 2:30 and it was 2:35. "Sorry," the woman said at the door, and then she closed the door and bolted it from the inside. "Is there any other place around here?" William tried to ask through the glass, and the woman just walked away.

"Jesus," William said. "Okay, we'll eat in Fort Fairfield."

William's plan was that we would drive to Fort Fairfield to see where Lois had been on a float through the streets in her glory as Miss Potato Blossom Queen—I did not know why this was important to William—and then we would spend the night in Presque Isle—a city forty miles away from Houlton but just eleven miles from Fort Fairfield—"because it interests me since Lois's husband came from there" is what William said, about Presque Isle, and we would think about what we were going to do the next day when we drove back down through Houlton before getting our plane to New York that night. I mean we would decide what to do about the woman who lived at 14 Pleasant Street, William's half-sister, Lois Bubar.

═

On our way to Fort Fairfield there was suddenly much sky, and in a small way this thrilled me, because I had grown up with sky all around me. This sky was just gorgeous with sun but also very low clouds in places like a quilt, and the sun went in and out of these clouds, lighting up the pastures of green, and we passed a huge field of sunflowers. We also passed by fields with clover as a dark cover crop for nutrients that I knew from my youth would be plowed over in spring. It was interesting to me that I felt this small happiness at an almost familiar scene, that the panic of the isolation from this morning had changed into this. I felt a happiness, is what I am saying. And it made me think again about the memory of me driving as a young child next to my father in his truck.

As we drove along the road—again almost no other cars were in sight—William said, "I'm sorry for all that crap I did in our marriage, Lucy." He kept looking straight ahead at the road, he seemed relaxed as he drove, his hands were at the bottom of the steering wheel.

I said, "It's okay, William, I'm sorry for how weird I got."

And he nodded slightly and kept on driving.

We have had this conversation—almost exactly that—for a number of years since we separated, not frequently, but every so often it pops up: a mutual apology. This may sound strange, but it is not strange to William and to me. It is part of the fabric of who we are.

It seemed completely right that we should say this now.

"Let me text the girls," I said, and I did and they both got right back to me. Can't wait to hear everything!, Becka wrote.

We drove by two small houses that had satellite dishes. In the yard of a farmer, four long trucks stood, trucks that used to haul things; they had not been moved for years, grass was growing up all over them.

William said, "My father was in the Hitler Youth."

"Tell me again," I said, because he had already told me that, many years ago.

William said, "The only time that I can remember my father mentioning the war, there was something on television, what was it, that program about a German POW camp? It was supposed to be funny."

I did not answer this because I had not had a television growing up, and also because I had heard this story before.

William continued, "And my father said, 'That's junk, William, you're not to watch it.' And then my father turned to me and said, 'What happened in Germany is very bad. I'm not ashamed of being German, but I am ashamed of what the country did.'" William added, musingly, "He must have thought I was old enough to hear it, I was about twelve. And then he told me he had been in the Hitler Youth, that he had to be, and that he had not thought that much about it, and that he had gone into Normandy, but he wanted me to know he had been in the Hitler Youth. And he told me that he thought he would die in that ditch in France but that those four American GIs didn't kill him, and that he always wished he could find them to thank them. I mean he wanted me to know that he did not support—at least at the point he was telling me about this—what Germany had done. And I just said, 'Okay, Dad.'"

William shook his head as he drove. "Boy, I wish I had talked to him more about it."

"I know," I said. "I wish you had too."

"And Catherine Cole—she never told me anything more about what he thought of the war than what you've heard."

I knew that too, but I said nothing.

═

William's apology about our marriage made me remember this:

Many years ago now, when William first told me about the affairs he had been having, there was one woman he cared for especially, even though he said he was not in love with any of them, it was the woman he worked with—not Joanne—and it seemed to me that he might leave me for her. We went to England, the four of us—I mean William and I and the girls—because he'd thought I always wanted to go there, and so we went, but it was shortly before we went that I found out about this woman, and the other women too. But as I said, there was this one woman in particular. And one night in London when the girls were asleep I went into the bathroom and began to cry and William came in and I said, "Please please don't leave!" And he said, "Why?" And I said—I remember so clearly sitting on the floor and holding on to the shower curtain, and then holding on to his pantleg—I said, "Because you are William! You are *William*!"

Later, when I decided to leave him, William wept, but he never said anything like that. He said, "I'm afraid of being alone, Lucy." I listened but I never heard him say, "Please don't leave, because you are Lucy!"

After I left there was a time I called him and said: Should

we really be going through with this? And he said: Only if there's not something different you can bring to the marriage.

There was nothing different I had. I mean, I could think of nothing different to bring to the marriage is what I mean.

═

About authority:

When I taught writing—which I did for many years—I talked about authority. I told the students that what was most important was the authority they went to the page with.

And when I saw that photograph of Wilhelm Gerhardt in the library I thought: Oh, there is authority. I understood immediately why Catherine had fallen in love with him. It was not just his looks, it was the *way* he looked, as though he would do what he was told but no one would ever have his soul. I could imagine him playing the piano and then walking out the door. And—slowly—I realized this: This authority was why I had fallen in love with William. We crave authority. We do. No matter what anyone says, we crave that sense of authority. Of believing that in the presence of this person we are safe.

And even through our Difficulties—as I had come to call them—William never lost this authority. Even as I thought of us as being Hansel and Gretel lost in the woods, I always felt safe in his presence. What is it about a person that makes us feel this way? It is hard to say. But when I met William, even after I married him, even after we were having our Difficulties, I still felt it. I remember when I was first married to him, and we had our immediate problems (as I have said), I said to a friend, "It is like I was a fish swimming round and round and then I bumped into this *rock*."

═

We passed a sign that said: Welcome to Friendly Fort Fairfield.

William leaned forward to peer through the windshield. "Jesus Christ," he said.

I said, "Yeah. My God."

Everything in the town was closed. There was not a car on the street, and there was a place that said Village Commons—an entire building—with a sign on it: FOR LEASE. There was a big First National Bank with pillars; it had planks nailed across its doors. Store after store had been boarded up. Only a small post office by the end of Main Street seemed open. There was a river that ran behind Main Street.

"Lucy, what *happened*?"

"I have no idea." But it was a really spooky place. Not a

coffee shop, not a dress store or a drugstore, there was absolutely nothing open in that town, and we drove back up Main Street again where there was not a car in sight, and then we left.

"This state is in trouble," William said, but I could see that he was shaken. I was shaken myself.

"I'm really hungry," I said. There was not even a gas station in sight.

"Let's head to Presque Isle," William said. I asked how far away it was and he said about eleven miles—but we were not on the turnpike—and I said I didn't think I could wait that long to eat. "Well, keep your eyes open and we'll stop if we see a place," he said.

We drove along for a while, and I said, "Why did you want to see Fort Fairfield so badly?"

And William didn't say anything for a moment, just kept looking through the windshield, biting on his mustache. Then he said, "I thought when I met Lois Bubar I could tell her that we had gone to Fort Fairfield to see where she had been Miss Potato Blossom Queen, that she would think it showed a real interest in her, that it would make her feel nice."

Oh William, I thought.

Oh William.

═

And then William said, "Wait. Richard Baxter came from Maine."

When I first met William, he told me about the work of Richard Baxter. Richard Baxter had been a parasitologist—he specialized in tropical diseases, as William did—and Baxter had found a way to diagnose Chagas disease; they already knew how to diagnose it, but by the time the diagnosis was made the person was often dead, and Richard Baxter had figured out a way to speed up the diagnosis. He had discovered—if I understand this correctly—that if you looked at the coagulated blood you could find the parasites. William had been working on Chagas disease when I first met him at that college outside Chicago, and Baxter had made his discovery about how to more quickly diagnose the disease about ten years earlier.

William pulled over and brought out his iPad, which he consulted for a few minutes, and then he said "Okay" and took a right and we were driving along a different road now. William said, "He was an unsung hero, that man. He saved lives, Lucy."

"I know. You've told me that," I said.

"He did his work at the University of New Hampshire, but he came from Maine. I just remembered that about him."

I looked around at the fields we were passing, and up on a small hill was a horse-drawn wagon driven by a man wearing a big hat. "Look at that," I said.

"It's the Amish," William said. "They've moved here from Pennsylvania to farm. I was reading about them."

Then we passed by a farmhouse, and on the front porch were two children. There was a small boy who also had on a big hat, and there was a small girl who wore a long dress and a small bonnet thing over her hair. They waved to us vigorously. So vigorously they waved!

"Oh, it makes me sick," I said, waving back at them.

William said, "Why? They're just doing their thing."

"Well, their thing is crazy. And the kids are forced to be a part of it." As I said this, I realized that it reminded me of my own youth, coming from the family that I came from. And David had come from a different background, but the insularity was similar.

Recently—back in New York—I had been watching a documentary on people who had left the Hasidic community, I had been watching this because of my husband who had died, and I had to stop watching halfway through. It's because it made me think so much about myself—not the world these people had left, that was not familiar to me at all, but how they were in the world *once* they had left. They knew nothing of popular culture at all, and this was true of David when he left, and it was true in my case as well—and it is still true in my case, because these deprivations never leave us.

"I mean I can't stand it because those kids don't have a chance," I said, flicking a hand back toward the house we had just passed.

William didn't answer. I could tell he was not thinking about the Amish. After a few minutes he said, "What a strange thing to come from this place and to end up specializing in tropical diseases." I waited but he said no more.

So I said, "How is your work going, William?"

He glanced over at me. "It's not going anywhere," he said. "I'm done."

"No, you're not done," I said.

"I'm done."

I didn't answer this. We were silent for a while as we drove along the road that went to Presque Isle. "*God*, I need food," I said, because my head was feeling strange, detached, as it gets when I need food.

William said, "And where do you suggest we find this food?" It was true that there were no places at all; we were going by trees and almost no houses, and this was the way it was for miles.

I glanced out my side window at the endless pavement with the dried grasses at its edge and I asked, "Are you jealous of Richard Baxter?" I have no idea why I asked this.

William looked at me quickly, and the car swerved just

slightly. "Jesus, Lucy, what a thing to say. No, I'm not jealous of the man, God." But after a number of minutes had gone by he said, "But you don't hear about any Gerhardt Diagnostic Methods, do you."

So I said, "William, you have helped countless people, you have done so much work on schistosomiasis—and you've *taught* people—"

He held up a hand to indicate that I should stop. So I did. I stopped talking.

As we drove, William suddenly made a noise that was almost like a laugh. I turned my face toward him. "What?" I said.

He kept looking straight ahead at the road. "Do you know one time when you and I had a dinner party—well, it wouldn't have been called a dinner party, you never really knew how to pull off a real dinner party—but we had some friends over, and long after they had gone home, way after, I had gone to bed, but then I came downstairs and found you in the dining room—" William turned his head to glance at me. "And I saw—" Again he gave an abrupt sound of almost laughter, and he looked straight ahead again. "And I saw you bending down and *kissing* the tulips that were there on the table. You were kissing them, Lucy. Each tulip. God, it was weird."

I looked out the window of my side of the car, and my face became very warm.

"You're a strange one, Lucy," he said after a moment. And that was that.

==

Each morning after David had done the breakfast dishes he would go and sit on our white couch by the window and he would pat the place next to him; he always smiled at me as I sat down beside him. And then he would say—every morning he said this—"Lucy B, Lucy B, how did we meet? I thank God we are we."

Never in a thousand years would he have laughed at me. Never. For anything.

==

As we drove I suddenly had a visceral memory of what a hideous thing marriage was for me at times those years with William: a familiarity so dense it filled up the room, your throat almost clogged with knowledge of the other so that it seemed to practically press into your nostrils—the odor of the other's thoughts, the self-consciousness of every spoken word, the slight flicker of an eyebrow slightly raised, the barely perceptible tilting of the chin; no one but the other would know what it meant; but you could not be free living like that, not ever.

Intimacy became a ghastly thing.

═

It was still very light out when we arrived in Presque Isle; the days were long in August, and it was not yet five o'clock. At least there was a town. But there were very few people around. One man sat on a bench on Main Street putting saccharin into a bottle of water; then he brought out a flip phone. I had not seen a flip phone in years. "Why are we here?" I asked William. "Tell me again." And he said, "Because this is where Lois Bubar's husband came from. Don't you listen?"

And I thought, Oh William. Jesus, William. This is what I thought.

He had been mostly silent on the drive and I knew he was in a bad mood. It was because I had asked him about his work; this was my thinking. And I had accused him of being jealous of Richard Baxter. But William's not talking had made me feel lonely.

The center of the town reminded me of a Western town, like in the olden days, I think because of the row of buildings that were not high that stretched down along Main

Street. We pulled into the parking lot of a hotel in the middle of the town, where William had made a reservation. This lobby was small as well—as the airport hotel's lobby had been—and the elevator was small and took forever to get to the third floor. "See you in a bit," said William, and he kept walking down the hallway, pulling his suitcase on its wheels; his room was one door down from mine across the hallway.

"I'm starving," I said.

"So we'll eat," he said, without turning around.

The room was a basic hotel room, but the lamp on the bureau was a huge blue lamp; I do not think I have ever seen such a big lamp. The room was dark because it did not face the lowering sun, and so I switched the lamp on. But the lamp did not work. I checked to see if it was plugged in and it was, but it did not work. From the window was a view of Main Street. The man was still sitting on the bench, but he had put his flip phone away. I did not see any other people. I sat down on the bed and gazed into space.

═

When Catherine was dying, I had spent the summer with her in Newton, Massachusetts, with the girls, they were eight and nine; I found a day camp for them there—and William came up on weekends. The girls made friends very easily, especially Chrissy, and because she and Becka were always, as I have said, close—though they fought a great deal at times—Chrissy's friends became Becka's friends as well.

My point is: I had my days free to be with Catherine—Catherine Cole, as William said whenever he called: "How is Catherine Cole doing?"—and Catherine and I, this is what I felt, made a nice pair. I was oddly (I thought) not afraid of death, and when her friends stopped coming to see her, as her hair fell out and she became so thin, it was mostly just the two of us, and Catherine hired a housekeeper to help with the girls at night. In my memory—except for when we first found out about her illness, she had shown up in New York to tell us, and she had been shaking, and to see her shaking like that had been tremendously distressing, except for that time, she did not seem to me to be unduly afraid, and much of the time—almost all of the time—in a way, we just chatted. I am not sure, thinking of this now, that I really believed she would die. She may not have really believed it either. She had treatments once a week, and we got it figured out: I knew we had one hour after the treatment before she would become ill, and so after the treatment we went to a diner and had muffins, and I remember Catherine eating the muffin, and drinking her coffee, but the memory I have of her is one where she was kind of stuffing the muffin into her mouth almost furtively—although I am not sure that is the right word—and then I would drive her back to the house in time for her to lie down and feel queasy; she never threw up, she just felt very bad that first day.

When William showed up on Friday nights, Catherine would often be asleep, and he would stand looking at her, and then leave the bedroom, and he did not talk much to me or, I think, to the girls during this time. In my memory this is the way it was.

And his not talking to me on the ride to Presque Isle made me think of this.

But Catherine and I had a rhythm going, and with the girls gone all day we would talk. As she became sicker she was in her bed more, and there was a big chair near the bed where I sat. It was not hard for me to do this, I would not want to give that impression, I loved the woman, and with my girls with us at night it felt exactly the right place to be. "Don't let them be afraid," Catherine said to me toward the end, as equipment was brought into her room. "Let them play with it," and in a way the girls did because (I think) they did not see their grandmother afraid, or me, and so they adjusted to the oxygen things that were brought in, and to the nurses that arrived toward the end.

—

Catherine's doctor spoke to me on the phone every day; he called with a regularity that I loved him for. He said: "This is not going to be pretty." And I said, "Okay."

I did not know how not pretty it would be, but that part did not last long. I told the girls that Grandma was too sick at the moment for them to see her, and they seemed to adjust to this. Their father came to them at that point—I mean William moved in full-time for those last two weeks—and I think he helped keep them calm. But toward the end it became horrifying.

One day William took the girls—it was a weekend—to a museum in Boston, and I saw Catherine becoming more and more agitated and it was heartrending. She was no longer someone I could talk to, she was a woman in discomfort, and although they gave her morphine—which she had rejected until the very end—she was still very distressed and unsettled that day. And I went in to see her, and she was plucking at the bedclothes and she was speaking in a raspy voice, about what I (sadly) do not remember except that it did not make a lot of sense, and I was just tremendously aware of her growing discomfort.

And so I made a mistake: I watched her and then I put my hand on her arm, and I said, "Oh Catherine, it will be soon now, I promise."

And that woman looked at me, her face was contorted

with fury, and she spat—she tried to spit—and she said, "Get out of here!" She raised an arm, a bare arm through the slit of her nightgown, and she said, "Get *out* of here you—you horrible girl! You piece of *trash*!"

I understood immediately that I had done the unspeakable, which was to imply to her that she would die. It had never occurred to me (at that time) that she did not know this, even as I (sort of) did not know this, although I knew it at the point I am speaking about. But when she said that to me, I went out to the side of her house where there was a faucet that came up from the basement, and there were pebbles there, and I sank down on them and I cried. God, did I cry. I cried as I think—perhaps—I have not cried before or since. Because I was young, and I had not seen this before although I had been through much, but—

Well, I am just saying I cried.

And I remember William coming home with the girls and he saw me by the side of the house, and he took the girls inside with the housekeeper, and then he came out and in my memory he was kind to me, really very kind without saying much.

When he went back inside the house he went to his mother's room for a few minutes, and when he came out he said to me, "No more visiting for anyone," and then I saw him sit down at the desk and start to write. He was writing his mother's obituary. I always remember that. The woman was not dead yet, but William was writing her obituary, and for some reason—for all these years—I have admired him for that.

It may be the authority thing I was speaking of earlier. I do not know.

═

I knocked on William's door, and when he answered it I moved past him and I said—we used to say this sometimes because of when Chrissy had said it as a little girl—I said, "Now listen, you're starting to piss me off."

But he did not smile. "Yeah?" he said coldly.

"Yeah," I said. I went and sat on his bed. "What's your problem?"

William looked at the floor and shook his head slowly. Then he looked up at me and said, "My problem. What is my problem."

"Yes," I said. "What is your problem?"

He went and sat down on the other side of the bed, turning to look at me. "Lucy, my problem is this. I told you my work was not going well, I told you that when you came over after Estelle left. I *told* you that. Then you asked me about it in the car, and I told you again. But you didn't listen. You completely did not hear me. And then you asked me if I was jealous of Richard Baxter. And—" He raised a hand. "It made me feel like shit. Which, frankly, I have been feeling like a great deal of the time recently."

We sat silently for many moments. William got off the bed and walked to the window and then back; his arms were folded across his chest. He said, "You know, you worry about Becka's husband being self-absorbed, only interested in himself, and I have to tell you, Lucy—you can suffer from that yourself."

I received this with a physical pain, like a tiny nail had been pushed into my chest.

He continued, "Of course I'm jealous of Baxter. I did nothing of significance in the field like he did." He turned to the window again. "And we come up here, and I'm scared to death about what to do with this Lois Bubar person, and you get hungry—which you always are, Lucy, you are always hungry, because you never eat anything—and so everything becomes about getting Lucy something to eat. And then when you mention my work, you asked me about my work, and then you immediately start talking about the Amish and what a cult they are. Who gives a shit if they're a cult or not?"

I sat there for a while and then I got up and went back to my room.

═

After I left William, and right before he married Joanne, and then after he did marry her, Chrissy became very thin. I mean she got sick. She had gone to college at the same place that William and I had met. And she got sick. She lost weight, and it was William who called me and said, "Chrissy looks skinny." I had thought that myself for a while, I had even mentioned it to William, but for William to say it made it suddenly real to me. He added, "Joanne thinks so too."

She was sick.

Our child was sick.

Chrissy was not talking to me much during this time. On Christmas Day they—all three, William and Chrissy and Becka (but not Joanne)—came to my apartment to see me, and Becka said, with tears in her eyes, "I can't stand you." She stood there with her arms tight beside her, as though to let me know I should not touch her. And then she said quietly after Chrissy went into the bathroom, "Look at her! You're killing my sister." She turned away and then back and said to me, "You are *killing your daughter.*"

William and I went to a woman who specialized in eating disorders, and she was incredibly depressing to speak to. She said that for someone Chrissy's age—twenty—that it was that much harder for them to come back, and then, as we tried to absorb this, she said, shaking her head, "It's very sad, because she is in pain. People don't do this unless they're in pain."

I remember that when we left her office, we were not angry with each other. We were both stunned, and we kind of walked around the streets not really knowing where we were going.

I have always a little bit hated that therapist.

I thought about this as I sat as still as a stone in a chair in my darkish hotel room. I thought about the fact that Chrissy had been that sick, and I think in a way for the first time I understood—I mean I understood this *fully,* with no mitigating in my mind, is what I am saying—that it had been my fault. Because I was the one who had walked out on the family.

I am not invisible no matter how deeply I feel that I am.

And then I remembered how during this time I had traveled alone to the college to speak to the dean there; I had thought that someone at the school could help. And I was an idiot. Because the dean was very unpleasant to me, she was really quite unpleasant, as she told me that when Chrissy got sick enough they would ask her to leave school, there was not one thing they could—or would—do for her. And Chrissy, during my brief visit out there, barely spoke to me; she was absolutely furious that I had contacted the dean. She said slowly, with her teeth almost clenched, "I cannot believe you came out here and saw that dean. I cannot believe you impinged on my privacy that way."

I want to say—I mean I must say this if I am going to tell the truth—that during this time I went every day to a church nearby that little apartment I lived in and I got down on my knees and I prayed—when I say I prayed I mean that I knelt and waited until I felt a presence of something and then I thought: Oh please please God let her be all right, oh please please please please let my daughter be all right.

I didn't bargain, I just asked. And always with an apology for asking. (I know there are so many other people who are terribly badly off as well and I am so sorry to ask for this personal favor, but nothing means more to me—please please please let my daughter be all right.)

When I was a child we had gone to the Congregational church in our town; we went every Thanksgiving for their free meal. My father hated Catholics. He said to go down on your knees was disgusting and that only small-minded people did that.

—

Chrissy got better, though it took a while. She went to a therapist who helped her, not the awful therapist that William and I had seen to talk about her.

Many years later, I spoke to a friend of mine who had been an Episcopalian priest, and he said to me, "Why do you think your praying for Chrissy did not help her?"

And I was astonished. It had never occurred to me.

But as I sat in that chair in my hotel room and thought of these things, I thought that what William had said was true. I was self-absorbed. And I remembered then that one time during those years I was having lunch with Becka in the city—she was home from college—and she was trying to tell me something (even now I can't remember what she was trying to tell me) and I interrupted her and began to speak of my editor; I was having problems with her. And Becka burst out, "Mom! I'm trying to tell you something and all you can do is talk about your editor!" And she wept then.

Oddly, that moment clarified something to me that day—and clarified it again as I sat in the chair in the darkening Maine hotel room. It clarified to me for a moment who I really was: I was someone who did that. And I never forgot it.

But I had just done it again to William. He had been trying to talk to me about Richard Baxter, about his own work—and he was absolutely right: I just rolled right over it.

For a very long time I sat in that room, and a very real pain—I mean I felt this physically—was in my chest, as though small waves of it kept rolling over and over inside my chest. When it became completely dark, I turned on the overhead light and ordered a cheeseburger to be brought to the room.

═

What happened then is what used to happen in our marriage when we fought. Whoever became the loneliest first would give in. And so William knocked on my door and I let him in—he had taken a shower, and his hair was still wet, and he wore jeans with a navy blue T-shirt, this is when I noticed his tiny potbelly—and he looked at the cheeseburger, sort of congealed on my plate, and he said, "Oh Lucy."

I said nothing.

I said nothing because I felt he had been right. I was embarrassed beyond anything I could remember.

"Lucy, forget it," he said. "Let's go downstairs and eat."

I shook my head.

So William picked up the phone and ordered room service. "Two cheeseburgers in room 302"—his room—he said, and then he said, "Two Caesar salads. And a glass of white wine. Any kind. Doesn't matter." He put the phone down and said, "Come back to my room, yours is so depressing you could kill yourself in here."

So I followed him down the hall to his room, which was cheerier—his lamp was working, and he had a large window that looked out straight to the sky, where the sun was starting to go down.

"Now listen," William said, and he sat on the bed next to me. "At least you're not mean."

"What do you mean?" I finally asked.

"I mean you're not a mean person. Look how mean I am, talking about the dinner party—and it *was* a dinner party, Lucy, you did manage those—and everything I just said to you was mean. Including about your being self-absorbed. You're not any more self-absorbed than any of us."

And I burst out, "Yes I am, William! I chose to leave you and Chrissy got sick—and—"

William, who looked exhausted, held up his hand for me to stop. Then he pulled his hand down reflexively over his mustache and stood up and he said slowly, "Chose to leave me?" William turned to me and then said with some vehemence, "Chose, Lucy? How many times does a person *really* choose something? Tell me. Did you really *choose* to leave the family? No, I watched you, and you—you just went; it was like you had to. And did I choose to have those affairs? Oh, I know, I know, accountability—I went to a therapist, just in case you think I didn't, I kept seeing that woman that Joanne and I went to, I went on my own for a while, and she talked to me about accountability. But I have thought about this, Lucy, I have thought about this a *lot*, and I would like to know—I really would like to—when does a person actually *choose* anything? You tell me."

I thought about this.

He continued, "Once *every* so often—at the very most—I think someone actually chooses something. Otherwise we're following something—we don't even know what it is but we follow it, Lucy. So, no. I don't think you chose to leave."

After a moment I asked, "Are you saying you don't believe in free will?"

William put both hands to his head for a moment. "Oh stop with the free will crap," he said. He kept walking back and forth as he spoke, and he pushed his hand through his white hair. "That's like—I don't know, that's like bringing in some huge piece of an iron frame, to speak of free will. I'm talking about *choosing* things. You know, I knew a guy who worked in the Obama administration, and he was there to help make choices. And he told me that very very few times did they actually have to make a choice. And I always found that so interesting. Because it's true. We just do—we just *do,* Lucy."

I didn't say anything.

I was thinking about the year before I left William how almost every night when he was asleep I would go out and stand in our tiny back garden and I would think: What do I do? Do I leave or do I stay? It had felt like a choice to me then. But remembering this now, I realized that also during that whole year I made no motion to put myself back inside the marriage; I kept myself separate is what I mean. Even as I thought I was deciding.

A friend had said to me once, "Whenever I don't know what to do, I watch what I am doing." And what I was doing that year was leaving, even though I had not yet left.

Now I looked up and I said, "And you don't choose to be mean, William."

"I kind of don't," he answered.

And I said, "I know that!" Then I added, "I'm really mean in my head, you wouldn't believe the mean thoughts I have."

William threw his hand up and said, "Lucy, everyone is mean in their head. Jesus."

"They are?" I asked.

He half laughed then, but it was a pleasant laugh. "Yes,

Lucy, people are mean in their heads. Their private thoughts. Are frequently mean. I thought you knew that, you're the writer. Jesus Christ, Lucy."

"Well," I said. "Anyway, you're never mean for long, you always apologize."

"I don't always apologize," William said.

And that was true too.

When the food came I realized he had—of course—ordered the glass of wine for me, and I was glad he had. We sat in two chairs in front of the desk and we talked and talked, we could not stop talking. We talked first about having come to Presque Isle: William said, "What was I thinking? I was thinking we'd walk around little neighborhoods and see cute houses and see where Lois Bubar's husband came from, but really, Lucy, what was I thinking? There's not a neighborhood in sight and I can't stand it here."

We talked about Bridget: She had seemed sad and sort of contrite when she came over the few times since Estelle left, she did not chatter her head off, and William said that was awkward and made him sad, and it made me sad as well. We talked about our girls and we both thought they would be all right; they were already all right but when you have children you worry about them forever, and then we talked about William's work. He said, "There's a life cycle to everything. Including a man's work." He really did feel that he was done. "But I'll keep going into that lab until the day I die," he said, and I understood.

William stood up and said, "Let's watch the news." He turned the television on and we lay next to each other on the bed watching. On the local news, a policeman's son had died of a drug overdose. There had been a car accident near the town of Jackman, a truck had turned over, but the driver had not died. And then the national news came on and the country, the whole world, was in disarray—and yet I felt a sense of coziness. Then William went into the bathroom, and when he came back out he sat down on the bed and said, "Lucy, maybe we should forget this whole Lois Bubar thing. I'm old, she's older. I mean, what's the point."

I sat up and said, "Let's decide tomorrow. Let's drive back through Houlton on the way back to Bangor, and we can figure it out then. But I know what you're saying."

He looked around the room and at the window, which was now dark. "I hate this place," he said. "So weird to think of Richard Baxter coming from such a place."

"Well, your mother came from here too," I said, and he said, "Jesus. You're right." And then William—running his hand through his hair—said, "You know, Lucy, when I was small my mother would get depressed."

"Tell me what you mean," I said. "I know she would speak of getting the blues. But she was always so cheerful when she said it." I reached and turned the television off with the remote control. I added, "I remember her one time, though, her telling me she got depressed."

William said, "I hated her after my father died."

I tried to think if I had known that. "Well," I said, "you were an adolescent."

William tugged his mustache. "I sort of forgot, but I couldn't stand her, Lucy. We'd have fights and she'd cry hysterically."

"Fights about what?"

"No idea." William shrugged. "Not the usual stuff. I mean it's not like I was out drinking every night or doing drugs. I don't know. But she would *bug* me. *God*, did she bug me."

"She was upset because her husband died," I said.

"Of course she was upset. I *know* that. I'm just saying that she was so needy."

I turned so I was sitting with my legs over the edge of the bed, and, facing him, I said, "I remember you told me that was the reason you took the position in Chicago—to get away from her."

William sat back down in his chair and stared into space. Then he said, "I wonder where she was when I was little."

"What do you mean?" I asked.

"When I was small, she'd get depressed. Like she said, she'd get the blues, that's how she put it. But I was thinking last night in that hotel room in Bangor, I was thinking how she put me in nursery school a year earlier than most kids went. Why did she do that?"

"Is that when you chewed on your collar?" I remembered Catherine telling me that when William was small he would come home from school with his collar chewed.

William glanced at me sharply. "It's when I cried," he said.

I waited.

"I'd cry every day at that place. And all the other kids were a year older than I was, they seemed huge to me." He waited, and then he said, "Lucy, I would cry—and the kids would circle around me at recess and they'd sing, 'Crybaby, crybaby.' "

"You never told me that." I was really surprised to hear this. I watched him, his white hair sticking up from his head. He looked so strangely familiar to me—I don't know why I say strange, but that is the feeling I had. "You never told me that," I said again.

"I'd sort of forgotten it. Except not. And I never told anyone. But last night it came back to me, that's why I thought about carrying Becka around when she was so small." William sat forward with his elbows on his knees. "Here's the thing. The teacher there, this woman—God, that woman was nice. She'd pick me up and carry me around. I remember her doing that, carrying me around."

I started to speak, but William raised his hand for me to stop. "One day my parents had to come in to see her. So they came there, to the little nursery school, and I went to play in another room. This was at the end of the day. They finally came to get me in that other room, and then on the ride home my mother didn't say a word, but my father was very serious, and he said to me, 'William, you have to stop having that teacher pick you up so often. She has a whole roomful of kids that she's responsible for.' Something like that he said, and I just remember feeling so *ashamed* on that ride home." William looked at me then. "That teacher never picked me up again."

I was absolutely amazed; he had never mentioned one bit of this to me.

William stood up. "But why was my mother even putting me in that place when I was so young? She wasn't working. Why wasn't I home with her?"

"I don't know," I said.

We spoke more about Catherine, about her feeling "blue," as she would put it. I didn't fully understand until then that this had been such a part of William's childhood. "Well," William finally said. "She was blue because she had left behind her kid." He added, "She left behind her little baby girl."

And he looked at me with such pain in his face.

Oh William, I thought.

Oh William!

That night he gave me a hug before he said, "See you in the morning, Button."

═

I could not fall asleep that night, even with the tablet that I have taken for years when I need help falling asleep. I kept thinking of William's observation that I was self-absorbed, and I did not know what to do with it; I was really uncomfortable thinking about it. I did what people do when they are accused. I thought of different people I knew and how self-absorbed they all were. Well, I thought, this one is so self-absorbed that he tries to hide it all the time and as a result he is not very generous, and that one is self-absorbed and she doesn't even know it. . . . And after a while I said to myself, Lucy, stop.

But my mind went various places.

I remembered this:

One day we were in Florida, the girls were around eight and nine, Catherine had died that summer. And we went to Florida in the winter for a few days—one of our first trips without her—and there was a place to do laundry in a building nearby where our room was, and I remember walking back from putting some laundry in, I was walking across a little lawn, and I was wearing a light-blue denim dress, and what I remember is that it was like a small bird flew through my mind. And the bird was this: a thought: Maybe I will have to kill myself. It is the only time I can remember thinking this. And the thought came and went like a small bird through my mind. I had no idea it would arrive. I have thought about this since, and I think it must have been that William had started his affair with Joanne by then and I did not know it but felt it. This is what I think.

Never would I kill myself. I am a mother. As invisible as I feel, I am a mother.

My own mother would threaten to kill herself when I was young. She would say, "I'm going to drive far away and find a tree and hang myself from it," and I was terrified that she would do so. She would say, "I won't be here when you get home from school," and each day I came home scared. And each day she was there. And then I started to stay after school, every day I stayed after school, I started to do this to be warm—because our house was so cold, and I have always hated being cold—and then I did it because it felt a relief to me to be there, and to be able to do my homework, and I also at times remember thinking about my mother,

Go ahead and do it then! Meaning, Go ahead and kill yourself. But I was worried that if she did we would become even odder than we already were in that small town.

After a few hours of these thoughts I took another tablet and fell asleep.

═

In the morning William looked exhausted, although he told me that he had slept very well. He was wearing his jeans and the same navy blue T-shirt, and he looked old to me. We went down to the small restaurant for breakfast and we were the only people there. But the waitress did not come over to us for quite a while. She was a middle-aged woman with dyed black hair, and she kept putting silverware into a tray and then straightening up near the coffeepots, and William looked at me and mouthed, What the fuck? And I shrugged.

When the waitress, pulling out her small pad and her pen, came over to us and said, "What do you want," I said I would like a bowl of Cheerios and a banana and she said, "We don't have any cold cereal."

So I ordered a scrambled egg and William ordered oatmeal and we sat there, kind of depressed but feeling okay, I think, I mean the place was not friendly and it felt strange.

After a while the waitress brought us our food, and then I said, "Pillie, did you ever have an affair with Estelle? I mean did you ever have an affair while you were married to her?" I was surprised that I asked this, that I even wondered this.

And he stopped chewing the toast he had just bitten into, and then he swallowed and said, "An *affair*? No, I might have messed around a few times, but I never had an affair."

"You messed around?" I asked.

"With Pam Carlson. But only because I'd known her for years and years, and we'd had a stupid thing way back, so it didn't feel like anything—because it wasn't."

"Pam Carlson?" I said. "You mean that woman at your party?"

He glanced at me, chewing. "Yeah. You know, not a *lot* or anything. I mean, I knew her from years ago, back when she was married to Bob Burgess."

"You were doing her then?"

"Oh, a little."

He must not have realized as he said this that he had been married to me at the time. And then I saw it arrive on his face, I felt I saw this. He said, "Oh Lucy, what can I say?"

"Did you do her when you were married to Joanne?"

"Lucy, let's not talk about this. But yeah, when I was married to Joanne. But with you—I told you at the time that there was more than one woman. And I also told you at the time that I was not in love with any of them."

"Forget it," I said. "It doesn't matter." And it did no longer matter to me, I thought. Even though a small sense of water lapping inside me took place as I said this. But I thought: So it wasn't *me* that made him do this, if he did this while married to Joanne and also to Estelle? Then it wasn't because of *me*? I could not believe this. And I thought about what he had said the night before about choice. He may not have had any choice about this part of him. How do I know?

I do not know.

"Let's go," William said, wiping his mustache when he was done with his oatmeal. He took a final swig from his coffee cup, but we had to wait again for the waitress to bring over the check. I watched to see if William would tip her generously, and he did, rolling his eyes at me as he pulled out the cash.

═

As we drove back to Houlton there was a lot of Queen Anne's lace half dried out by the side of the road. The sun was full and bright. We passed fallen-down barns where there were rocks in the fields, and we passed by a few white cows. William pointed out to me a field of unharvested potatoes: They were green on top, and he told me that they sprayed the tops to prevent the nutrients from going into the green part so the nutrients would go into the potatoes themselves. I was impressed that he knew that, and I told him so, and he said nothing. Across the road from the field of potatoes was a brown field of harvested barley.

And then we did pass some harvested potato fields, they were all brown soil and dug under. I saw how the potato barns were often built into a small hill. On the outskirts of Houlton was a motel called the Scottish Inn; it was closed down and had weeds coming up between its rooms.

"William, your mother had trouble sleeping," I said. This had just come to me now as I was recalling my night.

"She did?" He turned his head to look at me. He was wearing sunglasses; so was I.

"Yeah," I said. "You don't remember?"

"Not really."

"It's why she was so often napping on that couch of hers. She would say, Oh I just could not get to sleep last night."

"I guess maybe you're right. On those trips to Grand Cayman I would hear her up in the night and I always wondered what she was doing."

I looked out my window. We were passing by a field and also a line of trees that went along one side of the field. "I just remembered, that's all. Oh, *wait*." I turned to him and said, "When I was with her when she was sick, she would joke about not being able to sleep, and she said, It's time for me to take some pills, and then when I went to get them at the pharmacy—or maybe it was her doctor who told me this, *yes* it was her doctor who told me that she'd been taking sleeping pills for years."

"Great doctor-patient relationship," William said sarcastically. "Was there no privacy?"

"No, there wasn't. He liked me," I said. And this had been true.

We drove along in silence for a while, and then I said, "Well, I just think it's interesting. That she couldn't sleep."

"Lucy, *you* could never sleep," William said, and I said, "I know that, you idiot, and I know *why* I couldn't sleep—because of what I had *come* from—and I'm just saying maybe your mother couldn't sleep because of what she had left behind her."

"I get it," William said, and he glanced at me, but with his sunglasses on I could not tell how he was looking at me.

After another few minutes of driving, William said, "Lucy, we still don't know what we're doing here."

"Just keep going," I said. "Let's just drive by Lois Bubar's house and then we can pull over and think about it."

═

We drove into Houlton, and the brightness of the sun seemed to make the town sparkle—I mean the brick courthouse and the library, it all looked old-fashioned and very comfortable, as though the town had been comfortable with itself for many years, and the river sparkled too, and then we were on Pleasant Street.

And as we drove along Pleasant Street there was an older woman out in the front yard of the house we had seen the day before. She was bending over a low bush and she had a hat on and her hair was not short—I mean it was nice hair, sort of light brown, and it went to right above her shoulders—even though she was not young; but she had a youngish look to her as she bent over this bush; she was wearing a pair of brown pants that went above her ankles and she had a blue shirt on; she was thin but not skinny. I mean there was a litheness to her.

"William." I almost yelled this. "That's her."

He slowed down slightly and she did not look up, and then he kept driving and pulled over on the next block. He took his sunglasses off and looked at me. "Oh God, Lucy."

"That's her!" I said, pointing back in the direction of her house.

William glanced back and then he looked forward again. He said, "We don't know that's her. Lois Bubar could be sitting in a wheelchair in that house getting beaten by her son."

"Well, that's true," I said. And then I said, "William, let me go talk to her."

William squinted at me. "What are you going to say?"

"I don't know." But I said, "Wait here, and let me just go talk to her." I took my pocketbook with its long shoulder strap and started to get out of the car. Then I said, "Do you want to come with me?"

"No, you go," William said. "I don't know what to do."

Neither did I.

═

As I walked up the sidewalk I saw that in the side yard of the house was a clothesline that had strings of small rope hooked up between four large wooden poles. And in the front yard was the hammock that looked new, strung up between two strong trees. As I said before, this house was the nicest one on the block, it had fresh paint of a dark blue color and red trim. The woman stayed bent over the bush—it was a rosebush, and there were some flattish yellow blossoms on it; she was intent on whatever she was doing—and then I saw that she had a small spray bottle in her hand. As I got closer I slowed down; I did not know what I was going to do.

And then she looked up at me and sort of smiled and went back to the bush. "Hello," I said, stopping on the sidewalk. The bush was not far from the sidewalk. She looked at me again; she wore small glasses and I could see her eyes clearly, they were not big eyes but they seemed penetrating.

"Hello," she said, and she stood up straight.

"That's a pretty rosebush," I said to her. I had stopped walking.

She said, "My grandmother planted this years ago, and I'm trying to keep it going. It's got those damned aphids."

I said, "Yes, aphids can be a real problem."

She returned to her job, giving the spray bottle a little squirt.

So I said, "Your grandmother planted it? That's nice. I mean to have had it so long."

And now the woman stood up straight again and looked at me. "Yuh," she said.

I put my sunglasses on top of my head. "My name's Lucy," I said. "It's nice to meet you."

She stood there and I understood that she was not going to shake my hand, but not out of unfriendliness, it seemed, it was just something she was not going to do. She looked up then, at the sky, and then around the yard and then back at me. "What did you say your name was?" She was neither pleasant nor unpleasant.

"Lucy," I said. Then I said, "What's your name?"

She took her glasses off; they must have been reading glasses, I realized, in order for her to see the aphids, and she looked oddly both younger and older without them on. Her eyes had a bald look; I mean there were not many lashes. "Lois," she said. Then she said, "Where do you come from, Lucy?"

I almost said New York, but I stopped in time. I said, "I come from a small town in Illinois."

"What brings you here to Houlton, Maine?" Lois asked. She had a very small line of sweat near her hairline, right below where the hat met her skin.

"We're—well, my husband and I—well, my husband's father was a German POW here and so we came up to find out whatever we could about that." I switched my small pocketbook to the other shoulder.

"Your father-in-law was a POW here?" Lois looked straight at me, and I nodded. "Did he marry a woman from here?" Lois asked, and I said, "Yes, he did. And they lived in Massachusetts—then he died when my husband was fourteen."

Lois Bubar stood there with the sun beating down on her, and then she said, "Would you like to come in?" She turned and walked toward her side door and I followed her. Then she stopped and turned to me and said, "Where is your husband right now?"

I said, "My former husband, I'm sorry, I should have said that. We're friendly. He's sitting in the car on the next block."

She stood there watching me; she was not a tall woman, about my height.

I said, "He thought—"

And she turned again and said, "Come in."

We stepped through a dark mudroom where there were many jackets and coats hung up on pegs, and then we moved through to the kitchen, where she took her hat off and put it on the counter, and she said, "Would you like a glass of water?" I said that would be lovely, thank you.

So she filled two glasses of water from the sink, and I looked around without moving my head and I thought how much I have never liked the houses of other people. This house was fine—I mean there was nothing wrong with it, the kitchen seemed cluttered, but only in the way of a person living there a long time, and it seemed dark, after having been in the sun—I am only saying I have never liked being in others' houses. There is always a faint odor that is unfamiliar, and that was true in this house.

Lois handed me a glass of water—she wore one ring, a plain gold wedding band, I noticed—and we moved into the living room, which made me feel a little better: It was also sort of cluttered, but there was sunlight pouring through the windows and many bookshelves filled with books. On every tabletop in the living room were photographs, many photographs in a variety of frames. Glancing at them, I noted mostly photos of babies and little children with their parents, that kind of thing. There was a dark blue couch that looked saggy in the middle and an armchair that Lois sat down in, and then she put her feet up on the ottoman that was in front of it and I sat down on the saggy couch. On her feet were sandals made from rubber.

"Your *former* husband," she said to me, and took a sip from her water.

"Yes," I said. "My second husband died last year."

She raised her eyebrows and said, "I'm sorry to hear that."

"Thank you," I said.

Lois placed her water glass on the little table that stood next to her chair and she said, "Don't expect it to get any better. My husband died five years ago." And I told her I was sorry about that.

Then there was silence. She looked at me and I felt embarrassed, I felt my cheeks getting warm. She finally said, "What is it I can do for you?"

"Maybe nothing," I said. "I told you we came here to investigate my husband's—my former husband's—well, his roots, I guess you would say."

Lois smiled a tiny smile, I could not tell if it was friendly or not. She said, "Is he up here looking for relatives?"

I said, with a kind of small defeated sigh, "Yes."

"So your former husband has come looking for me."

"That's right," I said.

"And he's out in the car right now."

"Yes," I said.

"Because he's afraid," she said.

I felt defensive of William then, and also a little afraid myself. "He's not sure—"

"Listen, Lucy." Lois Bubar picked up her water glass and sipped from it again and placed it again very carefully down on the table. "I know why you're here. I even knew you were here in town yesterday, you and your husband were at the library. This is a small town, but you come from one, so you must know what that's like. People talk."

And I wanted to say No, because I lived in the middle of fields and hardly ever saw the town I lived in and no one in the town was ever nice to us, but I did not say this. So I said nothing.

And then Lois Bubar told me this:

"I have had a very good life." She held up her index finger and pointed it at me almost laconically. "I have had a very, very good life. So you be sure to tell your former husband that." She paused, looking around the room, and then she looked back at me. Her face seemed to me to be slightly guarded and even—just a little bit—bored. Behind her was wallpaper with flowers on it; there was a tiny water streak down it.

She said, "Let's just go straight to the point." Lois glanced up at the ceiling for a moment and then she spoke: "When I was eight years old my parents—together—they both sat me down and told me this, that my mother—well, they told me that day that I had had a different mother who had given birth to me. But they made it very clear that she was not my mother. My *mother* was the woman who raised me from the time I was a year old. That was my mother, she was brought up in this house"—Lois moved her hand slightly to include the living room—"and she was a wonderful woman. And my mother was so good as she told me this, and my father was too—he held me against him, I remember that. We were sitting on a couch and he had his arm all the way around me while they had this conversation with me. Looking back, I think they thought I was getting old enough to know this and that there were people in town who knew it, so they had better tell me before I found out from someone else. I was confused, the way any kid would be. But I didn't think it mattered.

"Because it didn't matter. I had two parents who loved me very much and I had three younger brothers and they were all loved as well. I couldn't have had a better mother and father, I really couldn't have."

—

Watching her, I felt she was telling the truth. There was something about her that seemed deeply—almost fundamentally—comfortable inside herself, the way I think a person is when they have been loved by their parents.

Lois took another sip from her water glass.

"As time went by, as I got a little older, I started to ask some questions, and they told me about the woman, her maiden name was Catherine Cole, said she had run off with a prisoner from Germany. She walked out of the house one day, walked right out, it was November, and she took a train and she never came back. I was not yet a year old. My father knew about the German, but he thought it was over by then. Catherine was very young when she had married my father, just eighteen, he was ten years older, and he said, he always implied, that she had married him to get out of her house." Lois paused and then she said, "My mother's name was Marilyn Smith—" She tapped the table next to her with her finger. "She was raised in this house and everyone knew that she and my father belonged together. They had been going together, and then they had a little spat of some kind and in swooped Catherine Cole—" Lois made a small gesture of her arms swooping upward; the water in the glass sloshed gently. "And my father married her. But Marilyn was right there for my father when Catherine left me—and him. She came over every day starting right after Catherine left, then they married when I was two. I suspect they wanted to look respectable, so they waited that year to marry. And of course the divorce had to go through."

Lois stopped talking. She put the glass of water back on the little table and then she placed her two hands together on her lap, and she kept looking at her hands. I kind of could not believe any of this was happening. In my pocketbook I heard my phone ping that I had received a text message and I pushed my elbow on it, as though to silence it, which was stupid. To the left of me I saw a photograph—not an old one, and it was larger than the others—of a young man at his graduation.

Lois looked back at me and she smiled that tiny smile again, which I could not tell was a friendly smile or not. A sliver of sunlight fell across her legs. She said, "Your mother-in-law introduced you to people by saying, This is Lucy, she comes from nothing. But do you know what *she* came from?"

I heard what Lois said, but it was like I had to run the sentence through my mind again. "Wait," I said. "How—how do you know that? About my mother-in-law, that she would say that to people?"

Lois said simply, "You wrote it."

"I wrote it?" I said.

"In your book—your memoir." Lois pointed her finger

to a bookshelf that was over to my right. Then she got up from her chair and walked over and brought out my memoir—it was a hardback—and as I watched her do this I saw that she had all my books lined up there; I was amazed.

"*Do* you know what Catherine Cole came from?" Lois asked again. She sat back in her chair; the book was balanced on the arm of the chair, and in a moment she placed it on the table near the glass of water.

I said, "Not really."

"Well," Lois said, with that tiny smile. "She came from *less* than nothing. She came from *trash*." The word was like a slap across my face. That word is always like a slap across my face.

Lois swept a hand down across her leg and said, "The Coles were a troubled family from way back. They just weren't much. Apparently Catherine's mother was a drinker, and her father could never keep a job. There was talk that he was abusive as well—I mean to the kids and his wife. Who knows. Her brother died in prison at a rather young age, I don't know what that was all about. But she was a pretty thing, young Catherine. I never saw a picture, of course, there were no pictures of her in the house. But they both told me that, my parents did. That she had been a pretty young thing. She went after my father."

Lois looked around the room. "As you can see, my mother—Marilyn Smith—she did not come from trash."

"No," I said.

Then Lois said, "Go drive by the place, it's been abandoned for years, but that's where Catherine came from, out on Dixie Road." She looked around and then got up and found a pen and she put her glasses back on and wrote down the address on a piece of paper. "It's off the Haynesville Road." She handed it to me and then she went back to her chair and sat down again, taking her glasses off. I thanked her. She said, as she seated herself again in the chair, "You should drive by the Trask farm, too, where I grew up. It's on Drews Lake Road, right over the New Limerick line in Linneus." She stood again and took back the piece of paper she had written on, and she put her glasses back on and wrote some more on it. "There you go," she said, handing it back to me. "My brother ran the farm for years, and now his sons do. It's all the same as it was. Nothing changes around here." She sat down once more.

And I was glad she sat down again, it meant she did not want me to go yet.

When I asked her, Lois spoke of being Miss Potato Blossom Queen; she said it had been fun—"Oh, it was nice, you know . . ."—but she said it had not been the best part of her life. The best part of her life had been her husband, who came from Presque Isle and became a dentist. She herself had taught third grade for twenty-seven years, and she had raised four children. "Every one of them turned out right," she said to me then. "Every single one of them. Not a drug problem with any of them, which is unusual these days."

"That's wonderful," I said.

"Have you any grandchildren, Lucy?"

I said, "Not yet."

Lois seemed to consider this. "No? Well, then you can't know how amazing they are. There is nothing like a grandchild. Nothing in the world."

A little bit, I didn't care for that.

Lois said, "I have one grandchild who is autistic, and that is a challenge, I will say."

"Oh, I'm sorry—" And I was.

"Yup. Not easy, but his parents are on top of it. I mean as much as one can be."

"I'm so sorry," I said again.

"Don't be sorry. He's very dear. And then I have seven other grandchildren, and they're all just great. Pretty great kids, they are." She leaned and pointed to the photo of the young man graduating. "That's the oldest one. Graduated from Orono a year ago."

"Oh nice," I said, and heard my phone ping again in my bag.

"Do you know," Lois said, "there are very few regrets I have in my life. And I think that's remarkable, because I look at the lives of the people around me and they are filled with regrets, or they ought to be, but I really feel that I have lived—as I told you—I have lived a very good life." There was, I saw then, a stack of women's magazines next to her chair, closer to the wall. The room, as I said, had a cluttered look, but it was not uncomfortable, and except for the water stain on the wallpaper behind her everything seemed clean.

Lois paused and stared off into the far corner of the room. "But one of my—maybe it's even my biggest regret—" She looked back at me then. "—is that when that woman—Catherine—came to find me I just wasn't as nice to her as I later thought I should have been."

"Wait," I said. "Hold on." I leaned forward. "Did you say when she came to find you? She came to *find* you?"

Lois's face showed surprise. "Yes. I thought you would have known that."

"No." And then I sat back and said, more quietly, "No, we had no idea that she came to find you."

"Oh yes. It was the summer of—" And she named the year, and I recognized immediately that it had been the summer I was in the hospital for nine weeks and had not heard from Catherine almost at all.

"Well, what she did," Lois said, and she crossed her ankles, settling herself into the chair, "what she did was she hired a private detective. Back then there was no internet, so she hired a private detective who found me—I was easy enough to find—and she knew this address, she came to this very house and sat exactly where you're sitting right now."

"I can't believe it," I said. "I'm sorry, but I can't believe this."

"Oh yes, and she did it on a weekday when she knew my husband would be at work, and the kids were all working at their uncle's farm—that's what the kids did back then, they all worked on the farm—and I had the summer off from teaching, and the doorbell rings—that doorbell never rings—" Lois pointed behind me to the front door, and I turned and looked at it. "And I went to that door, and she was standing there, and—"

"Did you know who she was?" I asked.

"You know . . ." Lois looked contemplatively at me. "I sort of did. Right away. But I also thought, No, it can't be." Lois shook her head slightly. "Anyway, she said to me, Do you know who I am? And I said, I have no idea who you are, and she said—she said this to me, that woman—she said, I am your mother, Catherine Cole."

Lois put her hand up and drew it slightly back. "And I wanted to say, You are *not* my mother, but I didn't. I just finally said, rather coldly, to her, Why don't you come in, Catherine Cole." Lois looked at me and nodded. "I was cold to her, I was really quite cold to her. My parents were both dead by then, they had died recently, six months apart—which she knew, of course, through the private detective—and I thought it was wrong of her to have found me after so many years, and also the way she just waltzed in and sat down as though she and I knew each other, and then she wept a little—"

"She wept?" I said, and Lois nodded and sighed with her cheeks slightly billowing out.

"But mostly she talked. And you know what else? She was very citified. I mean the dress she showed up in—well, I figured this out later, that she was sixty-two years old, because I was forty-one—and she showed up, in the summertime, in an *almost* sleeveless dress. Just little caps over the shoulders." Lois touched her shoulder with her hand. "It was navy blue with white—oh, what is it called, you know the word, what's the word, that stuff that goes around—"

"Piping," I said. I knew the dress that Lois spoke of. It was Catherine's favorite everyday dress. It had white piping around the sleeves and on the seams down the sides.

"Piping." Lois nodded. "And she wore no stockings either; the dress went to her knees, and it was just oh I don't know— It wasn't something you'd find anyone wearing up here. But do you know what bothered me the most about her visit? It was the fact that she only talked about herself. Oh, she asked a few questions about me—of course, she had found out most of the facts from the private detective—but she went on and *on* about—" Here Lois shook her head slightly. "Herself. Herself is what she talked about and how hard this had been on her."

Lois leaned forward and then sat back. "So I know about her not sleeping, and how she would get depressed—'get the blues' is how she put it, I think—and I know about her husband's death and her son; I knew that part from your book. Do you know she had the gall to talk to me about that man, her son? She raved about him, and, Lucy—I'm telling you—you would have thought he was the most brilliant scientist who ever lived. This was not what I needed to hear!"

Oh God, I thought. I said, "No, of course not." Then I said, "Oh, it's all she had at that point. Her son."

"Yes," Lois answered. "You're right." Her voice became quieter as she repeated "You're right." She glanced at her feet and then she said, looking up, "And I've thought about it since, and I think I might have shown her a little more compassion." Lois's face moved—I had to look away. Then she said, "But I will tell you—I got pretty sick and tired of hearing about her son. I really did."

—

After a few moments, Lois spoke again. She said, "She had told her husband about the fact that she had had this baby—me—and had left me, she told the German man. Gerhardt. And she said it had caused trouble in their marriage."

"So she *told* him?" I asked. "Did she say *when* she told him?"

"I'm not sure," Lois said, "I really can't remember, but it was somewhat early on, though not immediately. And all she said was that it had caused problems. I don't know what she meant by that."

Then Lois added, looking at me with her hand loosely held to the side of her face, "I'm surprised she never told you any of this."

"Lois," I said, "my husband didn't know about you at all until just a few weeks ago."

This evidently really surprised her. She took her hand off her face. "Is that true?" she said.

"It is," I said. "His wife, right before she left him, gave him one of those subscription things to find your ancestors online and that's how he found out about you. His mother never mentioned you at all—neither did his father. William never *knew*."

Lois appeared to be taking this in. Then she said, "My word." She shook her head. "Just a few weeks ago?"

"Yes," I said.

Then she said, "Did you say right before his wife left him?"

"Yes," I said.

"And you left him. According to your book." She glanced at the book on the table near her.

"Yes," I said.

"So he's had two wives leave him?"

I nodded. I wished I had not mentioned the part about his other wife leaving him.

After a few moments she said, giving me a quizzical look, "Is there anything—you know—anything *wrong* with him?"

I said, "I think he just marries the wrong women."

But Lois said nothing.

I felt bad for William, sitting alone in the car while I talked to Lois. I said, "Would you like to meet him?"

And she looked at me with a sad, almost closed-down expression and I realized she did not want to. She said, "I'm sorry. I don't feel up to that. I'm not young anymore, it's been pleasant enough speaking with you, but I don't wish to see him. No. I do not wish to meet him."

"Okay," I said. I made a move as though to get going and she stood up, so I knew we were through.

She walked me to the front door and pulled it open; it

opened with some difficulty, as though it was not often used. And I thought of Catherine coming through it now so many years ago, and sitting where I had sat.

I turned to Lois, and she raised her hand and just very lightly touched my arm. She said, "When I read your book—your memoir—I was so surprised to see that it had to do with the potato farmer, my father! And I kept thinking, She'll mention me in it, she will mention the fact that the woman left behind her baby daughter. But you never did."

"Because I didn't know that she had left behind anyone except her first husband," I said.

"Well, I know that now. But I didn't know it then. And do you know what? It's silly, but it hurt my feelings. It made me mad at Catherine all over again—and mad at you—because I wasn't mentioned in that book."

"Oh Lois." I felt a strange sense of unreality, and I thought my head was not quite working right, as though I needed food. Only more than that.

"Well." She laughed a small laugh. "If you write a book about this, I'd like to be in it."

"Oh my God of course," I said.

And she said, again with a little laugh, "As long as you make me look good."

As I looked back at her, the way the light fell against her

face, I saw then a fatigue on her face, and I understood that our talk had not been easy for her; it had taken a lot out of her, and I felt sorry.

═

I was almost not able to walk straight as I hurried down the street. And there was William sitting in the car. His head was thrown back on the top of the car seat and at first I thought he was sleeping; the window was all the way down. But he sat up the moment I stood near him. "Does she want to see me?" he said.

And I walked to my side of the car and got in and said "Let's go," and William started the car and we drove. The only thing I left out was that I had told Lois about his other wife leaving him, and her reaction to that.

Otherwise I splashed the whole story out to him.

═

William listened, interrupting several times, asking for clarification or for me to repeat something, and I did. Over and over we went like this as we drove, and William chewed on his mustache and squinted through the windshield, he no longer had his sunglasses on, and he seemed very intent as he listened. At one point he said, "I'm not sure Lois Bubar is telling the truth." And I said, "About what?" And he said, "About my mother coming up here. Why would my mother come up here at that point in her life?"

I started to say that I recognized the dress that Lois said Catherine had been wearing, but I didn't say anything, and William continued: "And Catherine's brother never died in prison. I have the death certificate for him online, and it does not say he was in prison."

I said, looking around, "Where are we going?"

"I don't know," William said. "Let's go find the Trask farm, and Catherine's house. You said you had the address."

"I have the address for Catherine's childhood home," I said. "The Trask farm is on Drews Lake Road in Linneus. No street number. But right over the line from New Limerick."

William pulled the car over and said, "Let's figure this out," and as he brought out his iPad I checked my phone and found two texts from Becka. The first said: Are you and Dad getting back together? The second one said: MOM, tell me what's happening up there??? I answered the first: No angel, we're not but we are doing very well together. And then I answered the second and said: So much to tell! I was surprised that she had asked that about her father and me getting back together. I put the phone back in my bag.

"Okay," William said. He had found Linneus, Maine,

on his iPad and he found Drews Lake Road, and then he started the car again and we drove, and after a while there it was: the house that his mother had lived in with Clyde Trask and where she had met William's father. It was a house. That's the first thing I can say. But I understood that in this area—in many areas—it was almost a stunning house. There was a long porch along the side of it, and it stood three stories high, with black shutters against the bright white paint of it, and there was a barn nearby that was stuck into a hill as these barns often were, and we pulled over and looked at it.

William said, "It's not doing anything for me, Lucy." He glanced at me. "I don't care, is what I'm saying." And I told him I understood that.

But we continued to look and we found the windows of what we thought was the room where the piano must have been where Catherine heard Wilhelm play, but we both of us, I think, felt a slight—revulsion would be too harsh a word—but we both of us, I think, did not somehow care for it.

And then we drove down the road, it was a road where nothing was on it, just a few trees being sprayed with sunlight right now, and then we saw a small post office; it looked very old. "Oh Lucy, look," William said, and I understood why this moved him. It was obviously the same post office his mother had come to check every day for letters from Wilhelm.

And as we drove slowly away, we were driving really slowly, we eventually came upon the railroad tracks and William said, "Oh God, Lucy. Wait a second." There right ahead of us was a very small station. Storage sheds were along the train tracks. As Lois said, nothing had changed. And as we pulled into the station—not a car was in sight, not another person was present—we sat there and looked at the road that Catherine would have half-run, half-walked down on her way that snowy November evening to the railway station. The station was small and clapboard. It was not as much a station as a stop.

Oh I could see young Catherine half-running, half-walking down that windswept November dark road, and getting to the train station without her boots, just her shoes and snow on the ground, and no real coat either, so that she would not be found out, and I saw her half-running and half-walking like this, in dark clothes with a scarf pulled over the top of her head, waiting at that train station, so frightened, so deeply frightened—as she had probably always been from her years of abuse at her father's hand—and I felt I could picture her thoughts:

If Wilhelm is not there when I get to Boston I will kill myself.

═

"Fucking Lois Bubar," William said.

I turned to look at him quickly. We were driving back along to the main road.

"I wish she never existed," he said. He pulled his hand down over his mustache and stared through the windshield at the road. "She wants you to put her in a book? And she wants you to make her look good? Jesus Christ, Lucy. And she says her only regret in her whole life is not being nicer to my mother? And then I show up and she won't even see me? What a piece of crap she is."

And I thought of the nursery school teacher who never picked him up again.

═

After my freshman year of college I got a job in the Admissions Department giving tours of the campus to prospective students. Oh, I loved it! I was so happy to have a job and not have to go back to my home for the summer, and I loved the college and I was happy to show people how much I loved it. But I mention this for one reason: There was a man who worked as an admissions person, he was not the director but he was at that time to my thinking a big deal, he was perhaps ten years older than I was, and he took a liking to me, and I only remember we went a few places together, but I don't remember where they were. He had a car, of course, though to me that was so grown-up, that he had a car, and I remember when I was first in the car and seeing that the door handles had cup holders in them, and I thought: Cup holders? It seemed *really* grown-up to me, and not exactly my style. But I liked him, I probably loved him. I fell in love with everyone I met. And one night when he dropped me off at the apartment I was sharing with a number of other student friends (friends!), he leaned me against his car and kissed me and I remember that he whispered, "Hey, Tiger," in my ear, and I thought . . . I don't know what I thought. But he was done with me after that night of just kissing, and a few months later he married the secretary in the office; she was a pretty woman, and I had always liked her.

I tell you this to explain how we kind of know who we are, without knowing it.

And the fellow in the Admissions Department knew I was not a person who could be with him and call him whatever a person calls someone after being called Tiger, and I could not really accept those cup holders; I was not sad to not hear from him again, it had always seemed a little strange that he would care about me in the first place. But again, my point! My point is: What is it that William knew about me and that I knew about him that caused us to get married?

═

The Haynesville Road was eerily quiet. We drove on this road for miles without seeing another car. There seemed, to my eye, to be a wretchedness to the road: Many trees were cut down on the sides of the road, and there were dead trees in swamps. In one place there were a few apples that were starting from trees, and William said that meant there must have been farms here at some point, and we kept driving. Everything looked a little burned by the sun.

A sign with a big Santa Claus head said CHRISTMAS TREES 300 FEET AHEAD. But we saw nothing in three hundred feet except for more of the same.

I could not stop the sense of fear I had in these Haynesville woods. There were many bogs with dead trees, and there was almost a pinkish glow to the different small dead trees, and a scrubby-looking weed that seemed almost like clover but not one I had ever seen before. We passed by a Baptist church—there was nothing else near it—and William said, "That could have been where Catherine and Clyde Trask got married, who knows." He did not sound like he cared, and I sensed that he thought his real mother was the one he had had all his life who lived in Newton, Massachusetts, and any woman who had lived up here was of no interest to him; this is what I thought I sensed.

And then—suddenly—alongside the road was a couch. Sitting by the side of the road was a small couch with printed upholstery; it was just there, and there was a lamp laid across the seat. But the couch was sitting where another smaller road went off the Haynesville Road, and as we slowed down to look at this couch I saw the sign for the road and it was Dixie Road. "William," I said, and he swerved the car onto this smaller road. The paper that Lois had given me said *Dixie Road, last house,* and as we drove down this road we saw no houses at all, and then we passed by one small house with a man standing in front of the house and he watched us drive by; he was old and he had a beard and no shirt on and he looked furious, I had not seen a stranger look at me with such fury since I was a child, and I was very frightened. The pavement ended and we passed by two small houses on our right and then after another long ride with no one around we found the last house on the road. It had been abandoned for years, it seemed. But it was the tiniest house I think I had ever seen. I had grown up in a very small house, and this one was much smaller. It was one story and looked as though it had two rooms. And next to it was a very small garage. The roof of the house sagged—it had been a flat roof, and the center of it seemed to be almost falling in—and the house was a maroon color.

And I could not believe it.

I looked at William and his face looked blank—stunned, I guess.

Then he looked at me and said, "This is where my mother grew up?"

I said, "Maybe Lois had it wrong."

But William said, "No, I found it myself in my research. Dixie Road."

We sat and looked at this place. A tree had spread its branches over the garage, and there were scrubby bushes that went up to the windows of the house.

The house was so—so—small.

William turned the car off and we sat in silence. Through the windows the inside of the house was dark; nothing could be seen. Only a little bit could I imagine people moving about in there. The grass had grown very high around the place, and saplings were standing close to it. Two saplings had even grown through the house, they came out of the almost-fallen-down roof.

I glanced at William and his face looked so bewildered, it made me ache for him. And I understood: Never in my life would I have imagined Catherine coming from such a place. Then he looked at me. "Ready?" he asked. And I said, "Let's go." And so he started the car and kept driving, the road was too small to turn around on, and it was a dead-end road, and at the end of the road, with much maneuvering, William got the car headed the right way and we took off. The man was still standing in front of his house looking furiously at us as we drove by.

The couch was gone from the side of the road.

"This is a horror movie," William said.

═

Our plane was due to leave at five o'clock, and we drove along the road to Bangor in silence. We passed by a restaurant whose paint was peeled, it had obviously long been closed, but in square letters out front was a sign that said: AM I THE ONLY ONE RUNNING OUT OF PEOPLE I LIKE?

After a while I said, "William," and he said, "What?" And I said, "Nothing." Then I said, "William, you married your mother." I said this quietly.

He turned his head toward me. "What do you mean?"

I said, "She was like me. She came from awful poverty and maybe a father—she was—I don't know what I mean. But you married the same sort of woman, William. When you had so many different people in the world to choose from, you chose a woman like your mother. I—I even left my children."

William pulled the car over to the side of the road. He stayed quiet and he looked at me. I almost looked away because it had been years since he had looked at me for such a long time. Then he said, "Lucy, I married you because you were filled with joy. You were just *filled* with joy. And when I finally realized what you came from—when we went to your house that day to meet your family and tell them we were getting married, Lucy, I almost died at what you came from. I had no idea that was what you came from. And I kept thinking, But how is she what she is? How could she come from this and have so much exuberance?" He shook his head very slowly. "And I still don't know how you did it. You're unique, Lucy. You're a *spirit*. You know how the other day at that barracks when you thought you were flipping between universes or something, well, I believe you, Lucy, because you are a *spirit*. There has never been anyone in the world like you." In a moment he added, "You steal people's hearts, Lucy."

William pulled the car into the road again.

I thought about this, and it seemed to me that as soon as I got into Mrs. Nash's car that day, such happiness had overtaken me. "Oh Pillie," I said quietly.

But William said no more.

═

And then William began to close down. I watched this happen. His face—it is odd—it is almost like his face remains but everything behind it retreats. You can see him going away, is what I mean. And his face got like that as we drove.

I said at one point, mostly to make conversation, "Ours is a very American story." William said, "Why," and I said, "Because our fathers were fighting on opposite sides of the war and your mother came from poverty and so did I, and look at us, we're both living in New York and we've both been successful."

And William said, without looking at me—he said this immediately—"Well, that's called the American dream. Think of all the American dreams that weren't lived. Think of that veteran with his car of trash we saw the first morning we were here."

I looked out my side window. Then I realized that the man standing in front of his house on Dixie Road looking at us with such fury was old enough that he could have been a veteran of the Vietnam War, maybe that was his story. I have told you before how I barely knew about the Vietnam War; we were so isolated as I grew up, and I was just young enough to not know anyone who was in it. But when I went to college and met William this changed, and I said, now, "You were so lucky about Vietnam, William. To get such a good draft number. Think how different your life might have been."

"I've thought about that my entire life," William said. And then he said no more.

It came to me then that I had possibly taken something from William by being the one to go in and see Lois Bubar. That had I just waited a few moments and thought it through, and had him come with me, she might have been just as pleasant to him as she was to me. This thought bothered me as I watched William driving with his face closed down. I thought how the first thing he had said was: "Does she want to see me?"

And I had had to tell him no. And his face, that slight bafflement that crosses it sometimes. I thought: Here is one more woman—in his mind—who has rejected him. And I thought once more of the nursery school teacher who had never picked him up again after having made him feel so special. And then I thought that maybe he had been sent to the nursery school because his mother had told his father about the baby and their marriage had trouble in it, and maybe Catherine had not been really capable of caring for him at that time. This made some sense to me.

—

So I said to him, "William, I'm sorry I just ran out of the car and was the one who got to see her. I should have had you come with me, I just ran right out—"

He glanced over at me and said, "Oh Lucy, who cares. Seriously. Who cares that I didn't see her. I was scared and you were trying to help." After another minute he added, "I wouldn't worry about that. Sheesh."

But his face remained the same.

═

We pulled into the airport parking lot, such a huge and empty parking lot. It took us a few turns to figure out where to drop the car off, even in all that emptiness, and we got out our suitcases and headed inside the airport. It was even—to my mind—stranger than it had been the night we flew in. It was small. But it was foreign, this is what I thought as we went into it. There was no place in it to get anything to eat. It was midafternoon.

As we walked through the airport—we had not yet gone through security—William said, "You know, Lucy, I need to just go walk for a bit." And I looked at him and said, "Okay, do you want company?" And he shook his head. "Leave your suitcase with me," I said.

But I was hungry and there was no place in the airport

to get food, so I went—with both our suitcases—back over the little bridge to the airport hotel and I walked through the double doors and saw right away that their restaurant was closed. Open at 5:00, a sign said. I gave a huge sigh and turned around to head back, and I thought to myself: When does anybody in this state eat? And just as I thought that I saw the fattest man I have ever seen. He was coming through the double doors that I had just come through, and he had pushed one of them open but this was not enough space for him to get through. He did not seem old; he may have been thirty, I do not know. But his pants went out on the sides of him like a ship almost, and his face was buried into itself. I let go of one of the suitcases and I pulled the other door open for him and he smiled in a way that seemed to me to be ashamed, and I said, "There you go," and he said "Thanks" with a kind of shy smile and he went up to the front desk in the lobby.

I thought as I walked back to the airport—I thought: I know what that man feels like. (Except of course I do not.) But I thought: It's odd, because on one hand I think I am invisible, but on the other I know what it is like to be marked as separate from society, only in my case no one knows it when they see me. But I thought that about that fat man. And about myself.

—

From a window in the airport, I saw William as he walked around the huge parking lot: He walked up one side until I almost couldn't see him, and then I saw him walking back down the other way, and as I watched he stopped walking and he stood shaking his head again and again. And then he started walking once more.

Oh William, I thought.

Oh William!

═

As we sat in the seats in the airport, I noticed William's face again. I recognized that expression so well: He was gone. He said to me, "You tell the girls what happened, I don't feel like it." And I said that I would do that. We boarded the plane; it was a small plane and we could not find room to put our luggage above us, so the attendant—a pleasant young fellow—took it from us and said we could get it planeside, meaning when we got off the plane they would have it on the jetway.

William sat in the aisle seat because his legs are longer than mine, and we spoke about various things—he spoke in a flat tone, once more, about the fact that Lois Bubar had not wanted to see him—and then we settled in and the flight was not long. As I looked out the window at

New York City, I felt what I have almost always felt when I have flown into New York, and that was a sense of awe and gratitude that this huge, sprawling place had taken me in—had let me live there. This is what I feel almost every time I see it from the sky. I felt a rush of tremendous thanksgiving, and turning to William to say this I saw that he had one drop of water coming down the side of his face, and when he looked at me fully he had another drop of water coming from his other eye. I thought, Oh William!

But he shook his head in a way to let me know that he wanted no comfort—although who does not want comfort?, but he wanted no comfort from me—and as we waited for our bags on the jetway he said nothing and he had no more tears. He was just gone, as he had been increasingly since we drove to the airport at Bangor.

We pulled our suitcases to the taxi stand and William got into the taxi ahead of me and said, "Thanks, Lucy. Talk to you soon."

But he didn't. He didn't talk to me soon.

═

Riding over the bridge—in the back of my own taxi that evening—I suddenly remembered times early in our marriage in our Village apartment when I had felt terrible. It was about my parents, and the feeling that I had left them behind—as I had—and I would sometimes sit in our small bedroom and weep with a kind of horrendous inner pain, and William would come to me and say, "Lucy, talk to me, what is it?" And I would just shake my head until he went away.

What a really awful thing I had done.

I had not thought of this until now. To deny my husband any chance of comforting me—oh, it was an unspeakably awful thing.

And I had not known.

This is the way of life: the many things we do not know until it is too late.

═

When I stepped into my apartment that evening we came back, it was so empty! And I knew it would always be empty, that David with his limp would never walk into it again, and I felt unbelievably desolate. I wheeled my suitcase into the bedroom and then I went and sat down on the couch in the living room and looked at the river, and the emptiness of the place was horrifying.

Mom! I cried to the mother I have made up over the years, *Mommy, I hurt, I hurt!*

And the mother I have made up over the years said, I know you do, honey. I know you do.

I thought of this:

Many years ago, I saw a documentary on women in prison and their children, and there was one woman, a very large woman with a lovely face, who had her small son on her lap—he may have been four years old. The documentary was about how important it is to have children with their mothers, and this prison let the children visit with their mothers—at that time—in a new way. And this little boy sat on this woman's huge lap, and he looked up at her and he said quietly, "I love you more than God."

I have always remembered that.

═

I met the girls at Bloomingdale's that Saturday. It was wonderful to see them, and to see all the other people there as well. Usually in late August one thinks of all the rich people of New York having left for the Hamptons, but there were plenty of the usual types: women who were old and stick-thin with their faces stretched and their lips puffed up. I loved seeing them; I felt love for them, is what I mean.

I looked carefully at Chrissy, but she did not seem pregnant to me. She laughed at me lightly and kissed me and said, "The specialist said not to do a thing or worry about it for three months, and it's not three months yet, so I am doing what I'm told. So don't you worry either."

"Okay," I said. "I'm not worrying."

We sat at a table and they said, "Now tell us everything!"

So I told the girls everything that had happened on the trip and they listened carefully. They were amazed by what they learned about Catherine, as I had been. Then I said, "Have you spoken with him?"

They both nodded, and Chrissy said, "But he's being a dickwad."

I said, "In what way?"

"Not communicative. You know how he gets." Chrissy tossed her hair back.

"Well, I think he was really hurt." I said this looking from one girl to the other. "Look, he got a double whammy: Estelle leaving him and then this half-sister who didn't want to see him. He got a triple whammy, really. Because he also saw his mother's house. You guys, that house was so—so—awful. I mean he had no idea she came from such a place. No idea at all."

They had both seemed astonished—as William and I had been—when I had described the childhood house that Catherine had come from. "It's just so weird, I mean the woman played *golf*," Chrissy said. And I knew what she meant.

After a few more minutes, Chrissy, taking a bite of her frozen yogurt, said, "You know, we have a half-sister, Mom, and I feel really responsible for her. I wish I didn't, but I do."

"How is Bridget?" I asked.

Becka said, "She's in pain, Mom. It makes me sad."

"Have you seen her?"

And the girls said that they'd had a date with her a few days earlier; I was surprised to hear this, and touched. They had taken her to a hotel for tea. "She was nice to us," Chrissy said. "And we were nice to her, but she was sad. So it was hard."

Becka said, "Maybe taking her for tea was dumb. But we didn't know what else to do with her. We couldn't think of a movie. Maybe we should have taken her shopping."

"Oh God," I said. After a moment I said to Chrissy, "Why do you feel responsible for her?"

And Chrissy said, "I don't know. I guess because, you know, she's my sister."

"Well, it was very nice of you two to do that," I finally said to them, and they only shrugged slightly.

Becka said, "I'm sorry I asked if you and Dad were getting back together."

"Oh, don't be," I said. "I can understand the question."

And Chrissy said, "You can?"

"Of course I can," I said. And then I added, "We're just not going to, that's all."

"Smart," Chrissy said. And then she said, "It's so strange to think of Grandma being this Catherine person you're describing. I thought she was the most normal person in the world. I loved her." And Becka said, "I did too."

They spoke of memories of their grandmother then; they recalled her house and the couch that was tangerine-colored and how their grandmother would hug them. "She'd just squish me to pieces," Becka said. "I loved her so much." And I had to agree with them that it was strange to think of their grandmother having had this life that they knew nothing about, that neither I nor William had known anything about.

They asked me again about Lois Bubar. "But did you like her?" Becka asked, and I said, "Yes. Kind of. You kids have to remember, she had spent her life thinking that Dad knew about her. So really, given all, she was perfectly pleasant."

"On Pleasant Street," said Chrissy, and I said yes, on Pleasant Street.

Becka said, "This stuff is happening everywhere now. Because of those websites." And she told us how a person she knew had just found out he was half Norwegian; his father turned out to be a different man than the one he was raised with. His real father had been a Norwegian fellow. "Literally the postman," she said.

"Get out," Chrissy said.

But Becka nodded and repeated that the guy's father had literally been the postman. Of Norwegian descent.

I told them how their father said "Fucking Lois Bubar" when we were at that train station and picturing his mother running away. "It surprised me," I said.

It was Chrissy who said, wiping her mouth with her napkin, "It surprised you that he said that?"

"At the time it did. A little bit," I answered.

Chrissy said, "She's his half-sister who didn't even want to meet him." Then Chrissy added, "But Dad can be kind of juvenile. I mean I sort of understand why she wouldn't want to meet him."

"Well, she didn't *know* that he can be—juvenile," I said.

"Oh, I know, I know—" Chrissy nodded quickly. "That's not really what I meant."

Becka said, "But she's his half-sister, that would be the main reason to meet him."

Chrissy stared into space for a moment, and then she said to Becka, "Think how you would feel if Bridget came to us when we were seventy years old and said— Well, what if she showed up out of the blue and we had never met her and she said how wonderful Dad had been as a father?"

"I'm not following you," Becka said.

But I felt I understood. There was something about the jealousy that children feel.

I wanted to text William to say: Stop being a dickwad to the girls.

But I did not.

There was, for me, a sense of sadness as I said goodbye to them; we hugged as we always do, and we told each other we loved each other.

As I walked home that day I thought how the girls had taken Bridget to tea in a hotel. Given who Bridget was, given who they all were, this was not especially surprising, but I thought of that tiny house I had come from—oh, I can't really explain what I thought! But it was very strange to think that the children I had were already—in just one generation—so different, so very different, from me and what I had come from. And from what Catherine had come from as well. I don't know why this came to me with such force at that moment, but it did.

And then for some reason I suddenly imagined Catherine at the age she would have been now. It made me gasp inside to think of her as that old; it made me deeply sad, the way we get sad to imagine our children very old, the idea of their vibrant powerful faces gone pale and papery, their limbs stiff, *their time over,* and our not being there to help them—(Unthinkable, but this will happen.)

═

I have wondered why it was that as soon as Catherine died, I wanted my own name back. In my memory, there is a sense of my rejecting her, a sense that she had been too much in our marriage. But it was a long time ago, and I do not really know. But thinking this, it came to me that William had a dream after she died that he was sitting in the front seat of a car with her and I was in the backseat, and she kept banging into the cars ahead of her.

Oh Catherine, I thought—

When I was taking care of her, I liked it. I mean I liked taking care of her. I felt there was an easy intimacy between us. I think there was.

But after she died, her best friend—who did not come to see her once ever during the last two months of her illness—said to me, "Catherine really liked you, Lucy." Then she said, "I mean she knew . . . Well, you know, she understood there were . . . Well," and the woman tossed a hand in the air, "she really liked you." I did not ask her to explain what she meant, it was not my nature to do so. I just said, "I liked her too. I loved her." But I felt—and I still feel—a tiny sting of betrayal by Catherine. She had said something (almost?) negative about me to her friend, and I was surprised and sort of hurt.

But here is an odd thing: After she died I remember thinking, At least now I can buy my own clothes, and soon after she died I went and bought myself a nightgown.

═

I called William after two weeks of being home. I called him to see how he was doing, and he said, "Oh Lucy. I'm just getting along." It was clear to me he did not want to talk— Perhaps he was off to meet a new Pam Carlson? Or even the real Pam Carlson?— This was quite likely.

But I felt just awful. I felt as I had when David died, I had never stopped feeling that, but to be with William in Maine had been a distraction, I saw this now. A mere distraction from the pain of losing my dearly beloved husband.

Except he was dead and William was not.

And here is the truth: Every night as I rounded the corner to the place I lived in, after going to the store for groceries or after having seen a friend, I pictured William sitting in a chair in the lobby of the building I lived in, rising slowly, and saying, "Hi, Lucy." I pictured this again and again, thinking, He will come back to me.

And he did not.

═

It was not too long after this, September by now, that I ran into Estelle. There is a shop—for, well, I suppose, for fashionable people—on Bleecker Street in the Village, there are many such shops there, but there was one that I knew Chrissy liked and her birthday was coming up and so I went down to the Village and I walked into the shop, and I saw a woman glance at me and turn away, and then she turned back and it was Estelle, and I understood she had been hoping I would not see her.

"Hi, Lucy," she said, and I said, "Hi, Estelle." She made no motion to kiss me and so I did not move toward her either. Then I said, "How are you doing, Estelle?" And she said she was doing fine. I thought she looked older. Her hair was longer, and the sort of wildness of it that I had often admired seemed now slightly crazy, with it being longer like that; I thought it did not become her, is what I mean.

Then she said to me, "How's William?" And I said, "Oh,

you know. He's doing okay." I gave her a small smile; I was not happy with her.

"Okay. Well—" And she seemed at a loss for words, and I did not help her out. Then she said, "Chrissy and Becka, are they okay?" And I realized of course she wouldn't know about them anymore, except for whatever Bridget told her about them. Estelle said tentatively, "I know Chrissy had just miscarried right before I—"

So I told Estelle that Chrissy was seeing a specialist to try to get pregnant again, and Estelle said "Oh!" and put her hand on my arm. But I still did not help her out. Except I thought I should ask after Bridget, so I did, and Estelle said, "She's all right. You know."

I wanted to say, I heard that she's very sad. But I just stood there until she said, "Okay, Lucy, bye-bye."

And then, as she turned to leave, I caught a glance at her face and there was tremendous pain there, and my heart unfolded, and I said, "Wait." And she turned back, and I said, "Estelle, you do what you need to do and don't worry about the rest of us." Or I said something like that, I was trying to be nice to her after not having been nice to her.

And I think she knew it because she suddenly said, so sincerely, "You know, Lucy, when a woman leaves her husband everyone feels sorry for the husband, and they *should*! But I'm just saying"—And her pretty eyes looked around the store, then back at me. "I'm just saying it's not that easy for me either, and I know that's not the point, and I don't mean to make it about me, but I'm just saying, it's a loss for me as well. And for Bridget."

And then I almost loved her. I said, "I know exactly what you're saying, Estelle." I think she saw in my face that I did, because she put her arms around me, and we kissed each other's cheeks, and she said, and she was starting to weep, "Thank you, Lucy."

And she pulled back and looked at me and said, "Oh Lucy, it was wonderful to see you."

Two weeks later I saw her in the neighborhood of Chelsea, which I almost never go to, but I had gone to see a friend who had taken an apartment there, and Estelle was walking with a man, not the fellow at the party, with her arm through his—he seemed older, as William was—and she was talking excitedly to him, and it was easy for me to look away: I was across the street.

So there is that as well.

═

I thought about Lois Bubar. I thought how she seemed healthy; I mean she seemed inside herself, as I have said, in a way that was comfortable. Her house had been filled with those photographs of her family, and it had been her mother's house. This quietly astonished me, to think of her living in the house that her mother had grown up in, tending to her grandmother's rosebush. But why should it surprise me? I guess only because it was such a sense of home that she had, and I have never had that sense of home. Her mother had loved her, she had kept telling me that. And she meant of course Marilyn Smith, the woman who married her father. But Lois Bubar was not a woman who had seemed neglected for her first year of life. Catherine must have loved her. She must have picked her up and snuggled her, she must have worried over her first fever, she must have been quietly thrilled to see when the child had first pulled herself up in her crib to a standing position. She must have, I kept thinking.

And we will never know.

But I know that my own mother was not like that. And I know the price I have paid, which has not been nearly what my brother and my sister have paid.

When I was a freshman in college I had an English professor who had the class—it was a small class—to his house on many occasions. And his wife was there. Later I became friendly with this professor and his wife, and she said to me one day—I was a senior by then—she said, "I always remember the first time I met you at the house and I thought: That girl has absolutely no sense of her own self-worth."

My brother's story is too painful for me to record. He is a kind man who has lived his life in the small house that we grew up in. To my knowledge he has never had a girlfriend or a boyfriend.

My sister's life is also painful. She was feistier, and I think this may have helped her. But she has had five children, and the youngest did what I did: She won a full scholarship to a college. But after a year, she—my niece—came back home; now she works at the same nursing home as my sister.

My brother and my sister, I see it more and more clearly, as murky as it still is, these lives are not the lives of people who came fully from love from the moment they were born.

I am surprised—as my lovely woman psychiatrist was surprised—that I was able to love at all. She said, "Many people in your situation, Lucy, just don't even try." And so what was there in me that William had called joy?

It was joy.

Who knows why?

==

I think how when I was in college and I lived for a year off-campus—except that I was mostly at William's apartment—how I would walk by a house on my way to school and I noticed that the woman of this house had children, and I would see her through the windows, and she was pretty—sort of, I think—and at holidays her dining room table would be filled with food, and the children, almost grown, would be sitting around the table, and her husband—I assumed it was her husband—would be sitting at one end of the table, and I would walk by these windows and think, That is what I will be. This is what I will have.

But I was a writer.

And that is a vocation. And I think how the only person who ever taught me anything about writing said, "Stay out of debt and don't have children."

But I wanted those children more than I wanted my work. And I had them. But I needed my work as well.

So I think sometimes these days how I wish it had been different—and this is a silly thing, and it is sentimental and foolish, but it still comes to my mind:

I would give it all up, all the success I have had as a writer, all of it I would give up—in a heartbeat I would give it up—

for a family that was together and children who knew they were dearly loved by both their parents who had stayed together and who loved each other too.

This is what I think sometimes.

Recently I told this to a friend of mine here in the city, she is a writer too, and she has no children, and she listened, and then she said, "Lucy, I simply don't believe you."

A little bit, it made me sick that she said that. A secretion of loneliness came to me. Because what I had said was true.

═

I was not wrong about a possible Pam Carlson. William telephoned me more than a month after we had returned from Maine and he said, "Lucy, can you google this person?" And he gave me a woman's name and I googled her and immediately I said to him, "Oh no, she's not right—God, no." And he said, "Oh Lucy, thank you."

In the years when William and I were both single—between our various marriages—this is something that we would do for each other, give advice of this sort.

I cannot tell you exactly what it was about this woman he asked me to google that day that put me off, but it was a society kind of photograph, I mean she was in a long dress with other people, she was maybe ten years younger than I am, and the place she was in was well-appointed, but it was her face, her being—or something—that just put me right off, some entitlement I think I might mean, and William said, "I came on to her and now she's really pushing things forward with me and she had me over the other night and I just could not get out *fast enough*."

And I said, "Well, don't go back, she's not what you want," and he said, "Thank you, Lucy." He added, "She'll hate me now, because I pursued her, but once I got her—Oh God, I can't stand her," and I said, "Who cares if she hates you," and he said, "You're right."

So there was that.

═

There have been a few times—and I mean recently—when I feel the curtain of my childhood descend around me once again. A terrible enclosure, a quiet horror: This is the feeling and it was my entire childhood, and it came back to me with a whoosh the other day. To remember so quietly, yet vividly, to have it re-presented to me in this way, the sense of doom I grew up with, knowing I could never leave that house (except to go to school, which meant the world to me, even though I had no friends there, but I was *out of the house*)—to have this come back to me presented a domain of dull and terrifying dreariness to me: There was no escape.

When I was young there was no escape, is what I am saying.

Thinking this reminded me of a time right before David got sick when I was in the Deep South giving a talk, and the woman who organized the talk said to me on the way to the airport the next morning, "You don't seem very urban." This woman had been raised in New York City, and I could not tell what to make of the remark; she did not say it kindly, I thought.

But the moment she said it I thought of my tiny childhood home. What came to me immediately was a sprinkling of dismalness that descended, and I have thought about this since:

How in my later years that stench comes back to me, the way people sometimes act—to my mind—as though I had a smell they did not care for. Whether the woman who drove me to the airport that morning felt that way, I do not know.

As I think of this now, I remember Lois Bubar speaking of how "citified" Catherine Cole was when she met her with her bare legs and the dress with the piping on it, and I think: Catherine, you did this, you managed, you crossed these lines in our world! And I think in a way she did. Her playing golf. Her trips to the Cayman Islands. How is it that some people know how to do this, and others, like me, still give off the faint smell of what we came from?

I would like to know. I will never know.

Catherine, with her own scent that she always wore.

My point is that there is a cultural blank spot that never ever leaves, only it is not a spot, it is a huge blank canvas and it makes life very frightening.

It is as though William ushered me into the world. I mean as much as I could be ushered. He did that for me. And Catherine did too.

═

Oh, I missed David so much! I thought about how for two days before he died he said nothing, not even really moved, and when he died I was not in the room, I had left to make a phone call. I have since learned that this happens frequently with people: They wait until their loved ones have left the room so they can die.

But the nurse told me—she said—(oh God!)—she told me that David had spoken, his eyes had still been closed, but he had spoken. His last words were "I want to go home."

═

And I had thought that I had no real home with him—but I *had*! This was my home with him, this small apartment that looks out over the river and the city.

I was not sorry to be in it, even with my grief.

I suddenly thought of how he loved raspberries on his cereal every morning. Fresh raspberries: He would go to a farmers market that came into the city on Sundays and he would go every July and buy raspberries and we froze them so he could have them throughout the year on his cereal in the mornings, and I thought of one morning when he was to have a colonoscopy in four days, and the directions from the doctor had said no seeds for five days, and on that day, as we started having our cereal—this was one of my favorite parts of the day, sitting with my husband for our little breakfasts—he suddenly said, "Wait, I need my raspberries," and I reminded him of the directions from the doctor, and I saw his face fall—it fell like the face of a child who is sad, and oh dear God we know how sad a child can feel—and he said, "But not even today?"

And so I got up and got him his raspberries—every night he took a little from the freezer to have with his cereal the next morning—and I said, "Okay, you still have time," and he ate the raspberries on his cereal that day and he was happy.

I mention this because it is one of those strange memories that we have when a person we love so much dies: David had his raspberries that day and he was happy. But I remember this, and it makes my heart ache.

I will tell you just one more thing about David, and then no more:

I had gone to the Philharmonic for three or four years with someone I had been seeing. And I had noticed the man who played the cello. Because he was slow to get to the stage; he had a bad hip, from a childhood accident, I found out later (and have mentioned here before), and he was a short man and just slightly overweight, and when he came onto the stage, or left it—because I would sometimes stay to watch him leave—he always walked very slowly and unevenly and he looked older than he was; he had gray hair around a small bald spot. And he played the cello beautifully. When I first heard him play Chopin's Étude in C sharp minor I thought: This is all I want. Except I do not know that I even had that thought. I just mean there was nothing else in the world I wanted except to listen to him play.

—

After I was through with the man I had been seeing, I went to the Philharmonic on my own twice, and I went home after the second time and googled the cello player and it took me a while but I found his name—David Abramson—and I did not know if there was a wife. There was almost nothing about him at all except that he played for the Philharmonic. The third time I went by myself, I suddenly thought as it ended and as I watched him walk off the stage: I will go to him. So I found the stage door that he would come through, and he did come through it, it was October and not that chilly, and as he walked out I went up to him and I said, "Excuse me, I'm so sorry to bother you, but my name is Lucy and I love you." I could not believe that I had said that! And I said, "Oh I mean I love your music." And the poor man stood there, he was almost my height—which is not tall—and he said, "Well, thank you," and he started to move away. And I said, "No, I'm so sorry, that sounded crazy. I just meant I've loved your music for a few years now."

And the man stood there beneath the light of the doorway and he looked at me, I could see him looking at me, and he finally said, "What did you say your name was?" So I told him again, and he said, "Well, Lucy, would you like to have a drink, or coffee, or a bit of food? Whatever your choice would be?"

Later he said it seemed almost providential.

We married six weeks after that, and I was not worried—

as I had always been—about getting married again because of how strangely weird I got after marrying William.

With David Abramson, I did not get weird or strange at all, life continued with him exactly as it had since that night that I first met him.

═

I thought about William over the next number of weeks, and how I had thought that he made me feel safe. And I wondered why I had thought that, because it made no real sense. But things in life don't make sense. And I thought: Who is this man, William?

I also thought how he had, as I said to him that day in Maine, married his mother. But who had I married when I married him? I had certainly not married my father—

My mother?

I have no answer for this.

And I thought of the enormously fat man I had seen at the airport on our way home, and how I had felt like him: that even though I feel invisible I also feel I have been marked but no one can see it right away. And then I thought: Well, William was marked too.

This made me think of Lois Bubar, who had leaned forward slightly in her chair and asked me, about William, "Is there anything—you know—anything *wrong* with him?"

And I thought: Lois Bubar, you can go to hell. Of course there was something wrong with William! Which made me almost laugh. That I would react to her now as William had.

═

And then one morning—it was early October—when I came into my building after going for my walk along the river, William was there in the lobby. He was sitting in one of the chairs reading a book, and as I walked in he closed the book slowly on his lap and then stood up and said, "Hello, Lucy." His mustache was gone. And his hair was shorter. I could not believe how different he looked.

"What are you doing here?" I asked.

And he laughed—almost a real laugh.

"I have come to ask you a question." He said this with a slight bow, and then he glanced at the doorman and back at me and he said, "May I come up?"

So William came up to my apartment and he stepped inside with a tentativeness. "I forgot your place looked like this," he said.

"When did you see it?" I was really nervous, and I did

not know why, except that he looked so different with his mustache gone and his hair shorter.

"When David died and I came to help you with the business stuff," he said, and he looked around.

Oh God, I thought, of course.

"So what's the story?" I asked. "What's with this new look?" Putting my hand to my own mouth to indicate the mustache.

And he shrugged and said, "Thought I'd go for something different. Got tired of the Einstein stuff." Then he said, with almost an excited expression on his face, "I think I look like—" And he named a famous actor. "Don't you?"

It was many, many years ago that I had last seen William without any facial hair—we were young, practically kids. And now he was not young.

"Well," I said. "Maybe. A little bit." I could not see the connection between William and the actor he had just named.

Then William said as he glanced around again, "It's nice in here." He added, "Small. And messy. But nice." He sat down uncertainly on the edge of the couch.

"You look like your mother," I said. "Oh my God, William, your mouth is your mother's mouth." And it was true: His lips were thin, as his mother's lips had been. But his cheekbones were prominent in a different way, and his eyes, oddly, did not seem as large. I realized he had lost weight.

Sunlight from the morning was streaming through the window that looked out over the river.

William said, "Hey Lucy! Richard Baxter came from Shirley Falls, Maine. Not from up where we were."

I didn't know what to say, so I didn't say anything.

William said, "Remember you went to Shirley Falls?" And I nodded, and he said, "Well, I was researching him and found out that's where he came from. Cool, right?"

"I guess so," I said.

Then William said, squinting up toward me, "Lucy, will you go to the Cayman Islands with me?"

I said, "What?"

And he said, "Will you go to the Cayman Islands with me?"

I said, "When?"

And William said, "This Sunday?"

"Are you serious?" I asked.

And he said, "If we wait any longer we get into hurricane season."

I sat down slowly in a chair by the window. I said, "Oh William, you're killing me."

And he just shrugged and smiled. Then he stood up and slipped his hands into his pockets. "Look," he said, nodding downward and then glancing up at me almost childlike. "These aren't too short, right?"

The pants were khakis, and in fact they were a little bit too long. I said, "No, they're fine, William."

He sat back down on the couch across from me. "Let's just go, Lucy," he said. The sunlight was in his eyes, and I got up and closed the blinds.

"Man, you really are just killing me," I said, sitting down again.

And then he seemed to get sad. He said, "Sorry."

I watched him as he sat there with his elbows resting on his knees, looking down at the floor. And I thought: William, who are you?

But it was more than that: I had a slight trepidation run through me, and it was a strange feeling.

William finally looked at me beseechingly. "I wish you'd come with me, Button," he said.

His calling me that was odd. I mean it felt odd to me. Not natural or something.

I said, "What's the book you're reading?" And he held it up. It was a biography of Jane Welsh Carlyle. I said, "You're reading that?"

And William said, "Yeah, have you heard of it?" And I said I had read it and I loved it, and he said, "I know. I like it too, but I just started it."

"What made you choose that biography?" I asked.

And he gave a small shrug and said, "Oh, someone suggested it. Some woman."

"Ah," I said.

Then he said, "I thought I should start to understand women more, so I'm reading it."

This made me laugh, a genuine laugh, I thought it was funny. And he looked at me as though he didn't quite get what was so funny about that.

"The woman who wrote it is a friend of mine," I said. And he looked only vaguely interested.

Then he said, "Just come with me to the Cayman Islands. We'll leave on Sunday and come back Thursday. We'd have three days there."

"I'll let you know tomorrow," I said. "Is that soon enough?"

William said, "I don't know why you don't just say yes."

"I don't know either," I said.

And then we spoke of the girls. I said I was trying to have a vision like my mother had had about me being pregnant—only I was trying to have it about Chrissy. "But I can't," I said. "I don't know if she'll get pregnant or not."

"You can't just will your visions," he said, and that was true.

I said, "Well, that's true."

He said, waving a hand, "She'll get pregnant again," and I said, "I hope so." I almost told him that Chrissy had said he was being a dickwad, but this man across from me seemed different, strange without his mustache and his hair cut shorter. So I said nothing.

We kissed on the cheek and he left.

═

As I lay in bed that night, thinking of William and his face in my apartment, of our conversation, all of a sudden I thought: Oh. He has lost his authority.

It made me sit up.

It made me get out of bed and walk around the apartment.

But he had lost his authority.

Because of a *mustache*?

Maybe. How did I know?

I remembered this then:

A few years after I left William I was with a man who lived across the street from a museum in Manhattan. The man loved me; he wanted to marry me (he was the man who took me to the Philharmonic), but I did not want to marry him. He was a good man, but he made me anxious. And what I remembered was this: Always across the street was the tower of the museum. Every night—I was there maybe three times a week—a light was on in this small tower, and

I always imagined a person working there late; I pictured a man, youngish or middle-aged, or sometimes a woman, so interested in the work that he—or she—had to stay there late, and I was always moved by the loneliness the person must be feeling as he—or she—worked alone in the lighted tower of this museum. The comfort I took—! Night after night as I looked at those lighted windows in the tower of that museum I felt so comforted to think of this lonely person working there all night.

And only years later did I realize that I had never *not* seen the light, whether it was a Friday or a Saturday or a Sunday night, the light was always on, and so only many years later did I realize that no person was working there during the hours that I watched it, past midnight and at three o'clock in the morning, right until the light outdoors became bright enough so that you couldn't see that the light was still on. . . . Only many years later did I realize I had been sustained by a myth.

There was no one in that tower during those times.

But I never got rid of it—in my memory—the comfort that I had taken those many, many nights of my life, when I had left my husband and I was very frightened, and I saw the light on as I lay next to the sleeping man who loved me but who always made me nervous. And the light in the tower had helped me through.

But the light had not been what I thought it was.

═

And that was my story with William.

I could not believe this; it was a huge wave that poured over me. William was like the light in the museum, only I had lived my *life* thinking it was worth something.

Then I thought: It was worth something!

I sat in the chair and looked out over the lights of the city. You can see the Empire State Building from my apartment, and I watched that, and then I looked at the apartments that were closer to my own, always there were lights on in some of them.

And then I thought: Okay, I will do whatever I can do to pretend this has not happened.

I wanted to protect William from this understanding that I had just had. And I wanted to protect myself from it as well. Yes, that would be true, but I am saying, as honestly as I can, I did not want William to sense on any level that he had lost this with me.

But the Hansel and Gretel that I had carried throughout my life, it was gone. I was no longer that kid looking to Hansel as a guide. William was just—quite simply—not the person who made me feel safe any longer.

I knew there was no point in taking a sleep tablet. I got up and walked around the apartment and then I sat for a long time in the chair by the window.

I thought of our girls. I thought of how Becka was the one who needed him most: the sense of her father as having authority, although she had never used that word. But it touched me deeply as I sat and thought of her sweet, child-like face. And I thought of Chrissy, who also, probably, still thought of him that way; he was her father, after all. But she seemed—to my eyes—more prepared to deal with him than dear Becka had ever been. And who knows why? Who-ever knows why one child turns out one way, and another a different way?

As the sun began to come up, I texted William: Okay I will come. And he texted back immediately: Thank you Button.

Then I fell asleep.

In the late morning, I moved about the apartment, putting out clothes on the bed to take with me to the Cayman Islands. I kept stopping to sit on the bed and think. I knew of course why William had chosen to ask me to go there and not to some other place. I pictured myself sitting in a lounge chair next to his, in the sun, just as Catherine had done. I pictured him reading his book about Jane Welsh Carlyle while I read some book myself; I pictured us putting the books down to talk every so often, and then picking our books up again.

At one point, I sat on the bed and said out loud, "Oh Catherine."

And then I thought, Oh *William*!

═

But when I think Oh William!, don't I mean Oh Lucy! too?

Don't I mean Oh Everyone, Oh dear Everybody in this whole wide world, we do not know anybody, not even ourselves!

Except a little tiny, tiny bit we do.

But we are all mythologies, mysterious. We are all mysteries, is what I mean.

This may be the only thing in the world I know to be true.

ACKNOWLEDGMENTS

I would like to acknowledge the following people:

First and always, my friend Kathy Chamberlain, whose ear for what is true has been a very large part of making my career what it has become.

And my late editor, Susan Kamil, who believed in me in a way that allowed me the freedom to write what I needed to and wanted to.

I would like to acknowledge as well Andy Ward, my wonderful current editor, who took over with great grace; Gina Centrello, my advocate and publisher; my entire team at Random House, whom I have cared about deeply; my steadfast and unbelievably attuned agents, Molly Friedrich and Lucy Carson; my daughter, Zarina Shea, for her generosity and belief; Darrell Waters, my old friend who inspired this story; my friends Beverly Gologorsky and Jeannie Crocker and Ellen Crosby for listening to me; Lee and

Sandy Cummings, who were invaluable in assisting in the research of the German POW experience in Maine; the magnificent Benjamin Dreyer, for being who he is as my copy editor, "Dr. B." And also, Marty Feinman, for his support of my work all these years, thank you.

And to Laura Linney, who unwittingly and miraculously gave bloom to this entire book, thank you as well.

PHOTO: LEONARDO CENDAMO

ELIZABETH STROUT is the #1 *New York Times* bestselling author of *Olive Kitteridge,* winner of the Pulitzer Prize; *Olive, Again,* an Oprah's Book Club pick; *Anything Is Possible,* winner of the Story Prize; *My Name Is Lucy Barton,* longlisted for the Man Booker Prize; *The Burgess Boys,* named one of the best books of the year by *The Washington Post* and NPR; *Abide with Me,* a national bestseller; and *Amy and Isabelle,* winner of the *Los Angeles Times* Art Seidenbaum Award for First Fiction and the *Chicago Tribune* Heartland Prize. She has also been a finalist for the National Book Critics Circle Award, the PEN/Faulkner Award for Fiction, the International Dublin Literary Award, and the Orange Prize. Her short stories have been published in a number of magazines, including *The New Yorker* and *O: The Oprah Magazine*. Elizabeth Strout lives in Maine.

elizabethstrout.com
Facebook.com/elizabethstroutfans
Twitter: @LizStrout

To inquire about booking Elizabeth Strout for a speaking engagement, please contact the Penguin Random House Speakers Bureau at speakers@penguinrandomhouse.com.

ABOUT THE TYPE

This book was set in Sabon, a typeface designed by the well-known German typographer Jan Tschichold (1902–74). Sabon's design is based upon the original letter forms of sixteenth-century French type designer Claude Garamond and was created specifically to be used for three sources: foundry type for hand composition, Linotype, and Monotype. Tschichold named his typeface for the famous Frankfurt typefounder Jacques Sabon (c. 1520–80).